"The book is an imaginative but historica[l] Christian female leader, Priscilla. Priscill[a] window through which Ben Witheringt[on] Christianity's expansion throughout the [first] year-old Priscilla, in a voice speaking to her adopted daughter Julia, reminisces and explores the contexts for the New Testament itself, thus *Priscilla* functions as an innovative approach to New Testament introduction, and photos give the book a deeper appeal."

Scot McKnight, professor of New Testament, Northern Seminary

"Women disciples like Priscilla played an enormously important but often overlooked role in the story of the spread of the Christian gospel and growth of the Christian movements throughout the first century. Witherington—a career-long contributor to the righting of this imbalance—here presents a plausible account of one of those leading women, a coworker of Paul and a teacher and matron of the early church. In the accessible form of a flowing story, he immerses us in the real-life contexts of the players of the New Testament, from the smells and sounds of the industrial districts and tenements of Rome, to the rhythms of life in a Roman villa, to the bustle of the small shops that lined Corinth's forum. Along the way, the reader is introduced to the major contours of Witherington's reconstruction of early Christian history and how the majority of the New Testament writings fit in to that history— developed and defended in his academic books, but made winsomely accessible here in narrative form. Witherington has shown himself once again the master of the ancient ideal for effective writing, communicating what is useful through what is pleasant."

David A. deSilva, professor of New Testament at Ashland Theological Seminary, author of *Day of Atonement: A Novel of the Maccabean Revolt*

"Ben Witherington's *Priscilla: The Life of an Early Christian* is an essential resource for all Christians, and especially pastors and students. Too many pastors graduate from seminary with limited knowledge of women's leadership throughout church history. Unsurprisingly, opposition to women elders, pastors, and leaders is due, in part, to this stunning ignorance of the women who built the church beside the apostle Paul. An expert historian and widely published New Testament scholar, Witherington brings to life the social and spiritual realities of biblical women like Priscilla who inspire and inform our faith today. I highly recommend *Priscilla* in following Hebrews 13:7, 'Remember your leaders, who spoke the word of God to you. Consider the outcome of their way of life and imitate their faith.'"

Mimi Haddad, president of Christians for Biblical Equality International

"We know much more about the lives and experiences of men in early Christianity than women. Fortunately, Ben Witherington combines his vast historical knowledge with engaging storytelling to imagine the life of Priscilla. From the glimpses of her life we catch in Paul and Acts, we can be certain she led an extraordinary life. Witherington's work of historical fiction captures that life well, all the while helping readers to explore the world of the New Testament."

Nijay K. Gupta, associate professor of New Testament, Portland Seminary

IVP Academic

An imprint of InterVarsity Press
Downers Grove, Illinois

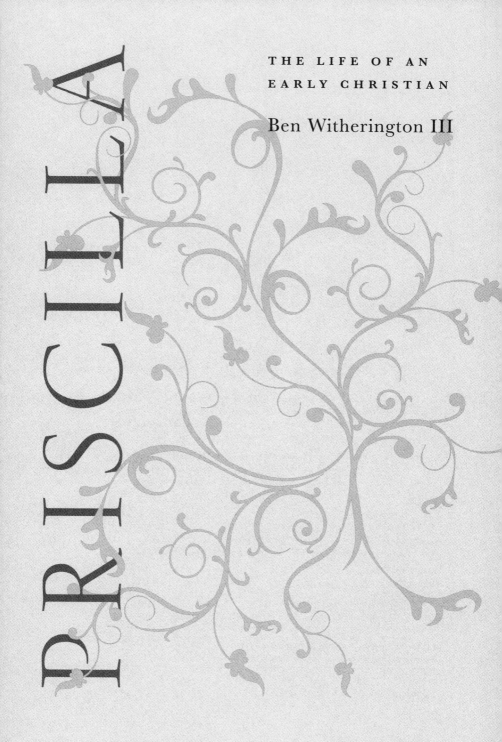

PRISCILLA

THE LIFE OF AN
EARLY CHRISTIAN

Ben Witherington III

InterVarsity Press
P.O. Box 1400, Downers Grove, IL 60515-1426
ivpress.com
email@ivpress.com

InterVarsity Press® is the book-publishing division of InterVarsity Christian Fellowship/USA®, a movement of students and faculty active on campus at hundreds of universities, colleges, and schools of nursing in the United States of America, and a member movement of the International Fellowship of Evangelical Students. For information about local and regional activities, visit intervarsity.org.

Cover design: Faceout Studio
Interior design: Jeanna Wiggins
Images: floral lines design: © vecstock.com / Shutterstock Images
      Greek orthodox icon: Godong / UIG / Bridgeman Images

ISBN 978-0-8308-5248-2 (print)
ISBN 978-0-8308-7086-8 (digital)

Printed in the United States of America ∞

InterVarsity Press is committed to ecological stewardship and to the conservation of natural resources in all our operations. This book was printed using sustainably sourced paper.

Library of Congress Cataloging-in-Publication Data
A catalog record for this book is available from the Library of Congress.

P 23 22 21 20 19 18 17 16 15 14 13 12 11 10 9 8 7 6 5 4 3 2 1

Y 38 37 36 35 34 33 32 31 30 29 28 27 26 25 24 23 22 21 20 19

FOR DAN REID,

A SCHOLAR, EDITOR, AND FRIEND.

Hope you enjoy reading this in your

newly minted retirement.

AND

FOR MY WIFE, ANN,

who has helped me with so many writing projects.

CONTENTS

ACKNOWLEDGMENTS

I wish to especially thank Alberto Angela for his wonderful chronicle *A Day in the Life of Ancient Rome* (Europa Editions, 2009). This novella would not be as informative as it is without his fine work. And also I should thank Andrea Giardina for his finely edited collection of scholarly essays by various experts titled *The Romans* (University of Chicago Press, 1993).

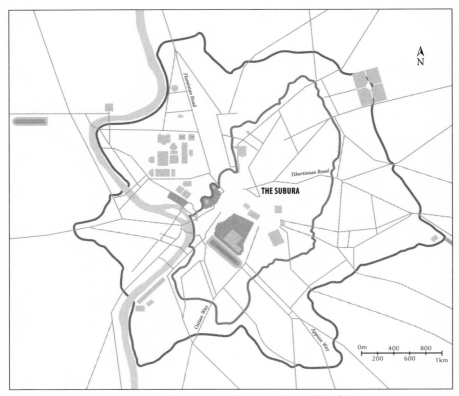

Figure 1.1. Ancient Roma with its districts. The *subura* is in the middle of the city.

FROM THE BEGINNING

All human efforts, all the lavish gifts of the emperor Nero, and the propitiations of the gods, did not banish the sinister belief that the conflagration was the result of an order. Consequently, to get rid of the report, Nero fastened the guilt and inflicted the most exquisite tortures on a class hated for their abominations, called Christians by the populace. Christus, from whom the name had its origin, suffered the extreme penalty during the reign of Tiberius at the hands of one of our procurators, Pontius Pilatus, and a most mischievous superstition, thus checked for the moment, again broke out not only in Judaea, the first source of the evil, but even in Rome, where all things hideous and shameful from every part of the world find their center and become popular.

TACITUS, *ANNALS* 15.44

ROME WAS BURNING, would not stop burning—trees and houses burning, the screams of adults and children, burning. For six full days, Prisca watched in horror as whole districts of the city burned to the ground, feeling despair as the *vigiles urbani* in charge of maintaining order and fighting fires fell with exhaustion, overwhelmed with their impossible task.[1]

The fire had started in the *subura* in an *officinae promercalium vestium,* or cloth merchant's workshop, where the stacks of flammable fabric easily ignited and grew to rage out of control for what seemed an eternity now. Yet those same flames engulfing the city had somehow only scorched the exterior wall of Aquila and Prisca's leatherworking shop.[2]

For days they'd watched the fire hoping it would spare their home as well, but then flames climbed right up the hill because of winds coming from the south, burning down the place where Aquila and Prisca lived in the *insulae*.[3] She wished she could have ignored her senses as she listened to the crackling of pine needles outside her window, that acrid odor of burning pine tar and wood. But then she and her husband were grabbing what clothes they could, snatching up a tent, screaming at everyone to get out of the house and head to the high ground of the Palatine Hill, the site of Nero's palace. As they made their hasty retreat from the flames, Prisca knew she would never outlive the memory of a lone dog whimpering in an entranceway to a villa, howling for its master, cowering on mosaic tiles that ironically read *cave canem—* "Beware the dog!"

Collapsing on the Palatine Hill, reeling from all they'd witnessed, what she couldn't help but hear next chilled her despite the blasting heat of the

---

[1] The *vigiles urbani* were a sort of combination of the police and the fire department. In an age before water cannons and fire hoses, putting out a raging fire required many people with many buckets of water, especially when a fire was in a city with the buildings made mostly from wood and closely bunched together.

[2] *Subura,* from which we get the word *suburb,* actually did not refer to an area on the edge of a town, but rather an area where many shops, tenements or apartment buildings, taverns, and the like were all crowded together in a small amount of space. The *subura* was where ordinary residents and resident aliens were apt to start their living in Roma within the central area of the city and not up on one of the famous seven hills, where a person of means could enjoy a good breeze and avoid the smells below.

[3] *Insulae* can refer to a city block, but it came to mean a city area where there were apartment complexes mostly in and around the *subura*.

Figure 1.2. Dog mosaic.

fire below them. The comforting plucks of a lyre. And singing. When Prisca lifted her head she regarded her emperor, Nero, his face lit by the flames while watching, enjoying the scene as if some drama enacted for him alone.

As she huddled with the others taking refuge on this higher ground, rumors began to spread as quickly as the conflagration through the Eternal City that Nero himself had ordered the fire set so that he could rebuild and remake it in his own egomaniacal image and even, some said, rename it Neropolis. However, barely had that rumor been kindled when Nero shifted the blame onto what he called that "atheistic sect that worshipped a crucified Jewish man named Christus."

And then the persecutions and martyrdoms in Roma had begun in earnest.

◆ ◆ ◆

Prisca tossed on her bed as the dream mixed with remembered images of the eternal flame in the Temple of the Vestal Virgins, that one light meant never to go out.[4] She snapped awake and pulled the blanket around her in the early morning as she struggled to banish the hellish dream of the devastating fire, in the tenth year of Nero's reign.

It's only a dream, she told herself. But even though it had happened more than thirty years ago, Prisca could not eject this scene from her sleep. Her unmarried, adopted daughter, Julia, who slept in the cubicle next to Prisca's sleeping quarters, struggled awake when she heard the rapid breathing.

"Can I help you? Is it the dream again?" her daughter asked with a concerned look on her face, rubbing the sooty sleep from her eyes.

Prisca nodded. "It happened again, Julia. The same nightmare. Again. After all our prayers and all this time, it's still impossible to erase the memory of those days. I've been thinking lately, perhaps it would help give me some peace, some rest from the nightmares, to put it all in perspective. Perhaps I should have you write my story. Maybe I should even go back to the beginning. When the Master died, and I was but a young girl visiting Jerusalem for the first time, during the Feast of Shavuot."[5]

Julia sat up straight, sloughing off the last of her slumber. She'd been in Prisca's household most of her thirty years and longed to know more of her mother's fascinating life, but until now Prisca had kept these details to herself, reluctant to relive them. Unable to hide her delight, Julia quickly answered, a torrent of words tumbling over one another. "I think it's high time you tell the whole story!" She got up and moved next to Prisca, speaking even more rapidly. "You are one of only a handful of Christus followers who are still alive and were there from the beginning. Peter and Paulus have been dead for almost thirty years, and the word from Ephesus is that John the elder is near death's door. I'll gather a stylus, my writing tablet, some papyri, and lots of ink. We can make a chronicle of how the

---

[4]Though occasionally it did go out, which would cost the life of one or another Vestal Virgin responsible, who would be buried alive as punishment.
[5]The Feast of Weeks, or Pentecost.

good news of Christus came to and spread throughout Roma, as only someone like you can tell it!"

Not feeling quite the enthusiasm Julia did, Prisca *could* see the wisdom of her words. As hard as it would be to replay all those difficult events, it was important that others knew what she had seen and experienced. And nothing else had banished the dream so far. Maybe this was the dream's purpose, to get her to put these experiences in writing. Silent for a moment, she sighed, and then nodded her head as she reluctantly replied in her worn, crackly voice, "I suppose you are right. After all, biographies of Jesus are being written, Paulus's letters are being collected, and various early sermons are being copied. Luke has even written his two historical volumes, but no one is telling the story of the church in Roma.[6] But we *must* begin at Shavuot, shortly after the risen Jesus had appeared to many and then once more disappeared into Paradise."

Julia sprung up and left Prisca's room to get her stylus and wax tablet; the papyrus and ink she wouldn't need until later. Prisca smiled at her young ward's eagerness, wishing she had more of her energy and zeal. "Well, I must dress for the day," she said as cheerfully as she could, rising much more slowly from her bed than the younger woman had. Going over to the *arcae vestiariae*, the clothing chest, she laid out her clothes for the day. Like most older matrons not abjectly poor, Prisca wore a long, ankle-length tunic. Over this she fastened a high-waisted *stola* at her shoulders with clasps, covering herself from neck to ankle with the thick wool.[7] As she looked at

---

[6] The name of the apostle to the Gentiles, in Latin, is *Paulus*; in Greek, *Paulos*. His birth name was *Saul*, named after the Jewish king, but being a Roman citizen, he also had a Latin name.

[7] The least expensive rough wool cloaks cost thirty-three times the daily pay of the weaver who made them, but a silk dalmatic could cost up to *twenty years' pay* of the silk weaver. See J. P. Morel, "The Craftsman," in *The Romans,* A. Giardina, ed. (University of Chicago Press, 1993), 233. Wearing expensive attire was not only a way of proclaiming one's social status but also of distinguishing oneself from craftsmen and the working class in general. Prisca did not like this manner of showing off one's wealth or making others feel inferior, not least because she too had been a craftsperson.

her simple garments, she had a moment of envy for the long tunics that rich women wore, made from expensive cotton or silk. She shook her head to clear the image, glad she'd heeded Paulus's advice about dressing modestly. She also eschewed makeup, though occasionally she would use some *pistic nard* perfume or ointment on hot days when going out.[8]

Prisca combed her streaked gray hair straight back, splashed water on her face from the small bowl on a stand next to her bed, and wiped her face with a small cloth. Since she wasn't going out today, she didn't put on her *palla,* or shawl, which she would drape over her head as another sign of modesty. She smiled thinking of Julia, who wore more colorful clothing and seemed certain that modesty didn't mean she had to be drab. Her daughter made a sharp contrast to the men of their household, who wore neutral-colored linen or wool. But Julia wasn't the only colorful highlight within the rooms of their home. Since they'd bought this house at auction, from someone with more lavish tastes, many colorful pastoral and mythological scenes still covered the walls. Prisca wasn't sure she liked them, but the bright imagery clearly brought great joy to Julia.

As she looked through the lattice at her window, taking in the scene below, the sun peeked over the horizon, illuminating the many lines on Prisca's face and the crow's feet around her eyes. She smiled as she watched the comforting signs of normal life at the beginning of a normal day.

Already the line for the dole of grain was forming in the square below. The carts rolled in through the gate, their oxen groaning under the load of grain and other goods. The cocks had been crowing for some time, and as with most Roman households, business had begun at six in the morning. Clemens, Prisca's *oikodomos,* or household steward, was by now sitting in

---

[8]*Pistic nard*, which shows up in several places in the New Testament (for example, John 12:1-8), was the Chanel No. 5 of its day. Women would even sometimes wear tiny vases around their necks to freshen up during a hot day, if they were out and about. There was as well what we would call lipstick, which Prisca does not use at all. The favorite sort was made of red lead and red mercuric sulfide, both rather toxic. Talk about the kiss of death!

the *tablinum,* and Prisca could picture the line of people snaking out the front door of the villa, waiting for a chance to speak with Clemens—the servants to get their assignments for the day, the clients to strike their bargains. The servants would be waiting for their *sportula,* or food basket, for the day as well.

At Paulus's urging, Prisca had freed the slaves who'd worked in her household long ago, but they loved their mistress and continued to work for her as freedmen and freedwomen, now paid for their labors, able to save their funds, get married—*and* they had become Roman citizens, under Prisca's sponsorship. Like them, Prisca was proud of her hard work and the quality of the leather products they made alongside each another.[9]

Prisca still owned the leatherworking shop down in the *subura,* in the center of Roma. Inscriptions and epitaphs, not to mention shop signs in the *subura,* attested variously to the presence here of a baker, there a shoemaker, an ironmonger, a wool merchant, a *purpurarius,* or dyer of purple cloth,[10] and yes leatherworkers, such as Prisca and her husband, Aquila, had been. Prisca chuckled remembering the time she and Aquila went to the funeral of a friend, Marcus Vergilius Eurysaces, who was a *panarium,* or baker. He'd had a mausoleum built in the shape of a bread bin, complete with images of workers in tunics grinding grain, kneading dough, baking and weighing

---

[9]There is clear evidence that craftsmen and women were quite proud of their work, despite the elites looking down their noses at them. For instance, we have an inscription on a tomb that reads, "Publius Longidienius, son of Publius, strives hard at his work," and above the inscription, the depiction of a man making a spar for a boat, standing on top of his toolbox. See Morel, "The Craftsman," 236. There is even clearer evidence of the snobbish attitudes of the Roman elites about manual laborers of any sort. See R. MacMullen's famous "lexicon of snobbery," where he collects all the belittling Latin terms the elites used to put down social inferiors, including craftsmen, in *Roman Social Relations 50 B.C. to A.D. 284* (Yale University Press, 1974), 138-44.

[10]This is where we get the word *purple,* and this trade was regulated and largely franchised by the Emperor himself, which suggests that the woman Paulus met in Philippi (see Acts 16:11-15), the Lydian or Lydia, was well-to-do, having become a successful *purpurarius.* Patrician Romans and especially royal ones wore clothes died purple, or a deep crimson, the dye coming from the murex shell—or in the cheaper version, from the madder root, which was especially plentiful in the region of Lydia.

loaves, while figures in togas, including Marcus, looked on.[11] He was a man rightly proud of his trade and the successful business he'd built.

Prisca shook the whimsical memory away. *I can never understand the snobbish attitude of patrician Romans who think manual labor is beneath their dignity,* she thought. *Thankfully I was not raised that way.*[12]

This same area in the *subura* included a synagogue that Prisca and Aquila had attended until they were expelled and exiled by Claudius for sharing their faith in Christ, some fifty plus years before. This same *subura*, where many foreigners took up residence as well, had become a meeting place for the followers of the Christ.

Nowadays, Prisca left the work in her shop to her freedmen and freedwomen, though she still managed the accounts. And the business was doing quite well, not least because the Roman army and the school of the gladiators who fought in the gigantic Coliseum built by the Emperor Titus, now some two decades ago, kept needing more tents, wineskins, sandals—anything and everything made of leather.

Roused from happy memories and from viewing the scenes in her mind's eye of what was happening as the day started, Prisca looked up as Julia returned, holding up her stylus and tablet. With characteristic fervor and a mischievous grin Julia said, "Let's get started! Never fear, as I will be able to keep up using old Tiro's system of tachiography."[13]

Prisca couldn't help but smile. "Very well. We must begin sixty-six years ago," she said, a faraway look in her eye that Julia recognized. "In some ways, it seems like only yesterday."

---

[11] This is true, and the tomb can still be seen today, near the Porta Maggiore in Rome. See Morel, "The Craftsman," 220.

[12] This attitude was indeed common among elite Romans; see for example, Cicero, *De officiis* I.42. He and Seneca both called work in a workshop "vile and vulgar." This was not the common attitude of Jews.

[13] So far as we can tell, it was Tiro, the scribe of the famous orator Cicero, who in the first century BC invented a system of speed writing, a shorthand that allowed him to take down verbatim whole speeches given in the Forum, in the courts, or in the Senate. Many thereafter copied Tiro's method, and by the late first century AD it was a common practice of literate persons and scribes.

2

THE JOURNEY TO JERUSALEM

The filigree flame of fire fell on the fellowship

Pursuant to the prayer and praise and paeans of the plaintiffs

Such that there was no room in the upper room,

And they fled like men fleeing a burning building.

But even the Temple courts could not contain the ebullience and effervescence

And so they were deemed drunk, tipplers before their time.

Yet all that they had imbibed was Spirit,

Which was so like fire in their bones that their wayward words

Leaked out in languages unknown to the speakers,

As if the babble of Babel had been set in reverse,

To unite a divided Empire that pretended Pax Romana.

Prisca sat in an upright chair in her bedroom, Julia by her side. Before they began, Prisca leaned over to pat Julia on the knee. "Thank you for pushing me to do this. It may be difficult for me. You know I'm not given to emotion, but there are times I may have trouble as I tell this tale. Mostly I've tried to forget rather than remember. Please have patience with me if I struggle some."

Julia leaned in to hug the beloved woman beside her—the one who had taken her in and made her a part of her family—the one who had given her hope when she had none. Her *mother*. She knew that Prisca had seen terrors Julia couldn't even imagine, and she was humbled to be given the opportunity to record these earth-shattering events.

Julia quickly released Prisca from her embrace. She could see tears pool in her eyes and didn't want to make her more uncomfortable, for rarely did Prisca show her feelings. She'd been through so much that she'd learned to steel herself against the horrors of life. Julia determined she would try to make this as easy on her as possible. Both sat awkwardly for a moment as Prisca quickly brushed away her tears with the corner of her sleeve and sat a little straighter. Clearing her throat, she began.

"I'll try to tell it to you as if you were a stranger," she said, patting Julia's knee once more. "I think that's the only way I can make it through this. It's best to start at the beginning. I was born a freedwoman, connected with the Acilian gens in Roma, and given my adoptive mother's name, Priscilla—Prisca for short. I was only fourteen at the time, but my mistress loved me dearly, as she had been unable to have her own children, and so I became the daughter she always longed for."

"As I am," Julia interjected with a smile.

Prisca nodded her head once, in patient agreement with her daughter's interruption, before going on. "Indeed. I went from being a freedwoman, to an adopted child, even to being a Roman citizen, so adamant was my mistress that I would be family and be treated as such. I went with her everywhere to attend to her needs, and that included the synagogue in the *subura,* which is where and how I came to worship the God of the Jews. You see, Priscilla had become a synagogue adherent, so earnest about her new faith that she begged her husband for permission to make a pilgrimage to Jerusalem to see the great temple Herod had built, to worship there with others who believed in the One God."

As Julia wrote, Prisca took up pieces of bread for both of them, realizing neither had broken their morning fast. She took a bite and chewed thoughtfully as she waited for Julia to catch up. When Julia looked up expectantly, Prisca offered her the bread, but her mother's story was what Julia had been waiting so long for; she shook her head no.

"Having seen none of the world outside Roma, I could hardly contain my excitement when my mistress told me we were going to Jerusalem to the festival. Old Festus, her much older husband, grudgingly let Priscilla and me go on the condition that we travel only during the regular sailing season, which meant between late Martius and early Octobris. His preference was early summer, when the winds would be favorable. So, to please her husband, Priscilla had to settle for going to the feast of Shavuot, rather than Passover, which was in the spring."

"Very sensible of him," Julia added with a decisive nod as she wrote.

Prisca gave a wry smile and said mischievously, "Old Festus was nothing if not sensible."

Julia looked up and grinned at her, appreciating that they shared the same dry sense of humor. For a moment, Prisca had a faraway look in her eye, as if she were transported to a different time or place. It gave Julia pause, and a bit of a thrill, as she anticipated what would come next in Prisca's tale.

"Large sailing ships then were mostly grain freighters and were the only boats that dared sail diagonally across *mare nostrum,*[1] and so we booked passage on the freighter called Apollo. We had to bring all our own provisions.

---

[1] The rather self-centered Roman name for the Mediterranean Sea. The Latin phrase means "our sea," as if it belonged to Rome.

The ship sailed from Puteoli to the famous harbor in Alexandria, a journey of some one thousand sea miles that took just over nine days. And that was just to Egypt! From there we had to book a much smaller commercial boat to Caesarea Maritima, Herod's port built to service the province of Judaea."

"Was the grain ship terribly uncomfortable?" Julia asked.

"Yes, it was very basic. Only the captain had what could be called a comfortable quarter. But I was young and excited to make the journey, so I didn't mind."

Figure 2.1. Caesarea Maritima Harbor today.

Julia nodded as Prisca continued. "From there we had to walk overland some sixty-five Roman miles to Jerusalem and find a wayfarer's inn or hostel where we could stay."[2]

Julia gave her a horrified look at the thought of such a long walk, but she bit her tongue and refrained from saying anything because she was afraid she'd interrupted too much already.

---

[2]A Roman mile was 4,800 feet, compared to 5,280 feet of a modern mile.

Prisca noticed Julia's alarmed expression, so she explained. "So many people were going up to Jerusalem there were no horses or camels available to ride. Priscilla hadn't taken into account what huge crowds came to these Jewish festivals—in this case something like four times the normal population of Jerusalem showed up for the festival, or about two hundred thousand or so people from all over the empire."

Julia's eyes grew wide as she wrote the figures down.

"We learned soon after arriving that a microcosm of the entire empire had shown up, and even some people from beyond the empire's borders! There were Parthians, Medes and Elamites; residents of Mesopotamia, Judea and Cappadocia, Pontus and Asia, Phrygia and Pamphylia, Egypt and the parts of Libya near Cyrene; visitors from Roma (both Jews and converts to Judaism like ourselves); Cretans and Arabs."[3]

Prisca's eyes focused on a table in the corner of the room, her mind revisiting that time. She could smell the odors and hear the sounds. "The cacophony of languages, the vast majority of which I didn't know, was overwhelming. I knew Latin and some Greek, thanks to the *paidagogos*[4] Priscilla had hired to watch over me and take me back and forth to school, where the great Herodes taught boys and only a few girls, myself included. I felt quite privileged," she said, her chin raised high.

Julia smiled with satisfaction, and a slight feeling of jealousy, as she absorbed what would have been any girl's amazing opportunity.

"I knew nothing of the Jewish language except a few words like *shalom*, for the synagogue in Roma read from the Greek translation of the Jewish scriptures." Prisca paused to allow Julia to catch up, and to change tablets,

---

[3] Acts 2:9-11.
[4] A *paidagogos* (see Galatians 4) was not a teacher. He or she was a slave who minded children, someone we might call a nanny. His or her job was to protect and accompany the owner's child back and forth to school and other places, carrying the child's scrolls and writing equipment, and then helping the child memorize and recite assigned lessons. Usually, a rhetorician (also preferably a good teacher of Greek) would be the actual instructor.

Figure 2.2. A Greek instructor with students. The *paidagogos* stands at the far right with the kit to hold the stylus and tablet.

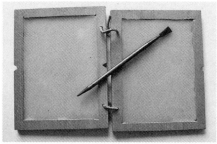

Figure 2.3. A writing tablet that uses bee's wax.

for already there were many words to this story. She thought perhaps they might need more tablets before they were through.

Julia wrote furiously. Later, she would read back the story to Prisca a bit at a time before composing a fair hand copy onto papyrus. The sounds of the day were increasingly coming into the house, and Prisca stood to see that Clemens had finished his meetings with clients and workers and was going to the back of the villa to check the vines in the peristyle's garden.

"I'm ready, Mistress," Julia said softly.

Prisca returned to her seat. "Excellent," she said, softly patting Julia's writing hand. "You can only imagine how overwhelming it was to visit a foreign city teeming with all different kinds of people. Fortunately, there were some other pilgrims from Roma who told us where we could stay—in this case, a hostel on Mount Ophel, in sight of the temple. The festival went on for several days, and we made a point of going to the temple on the morning of the second day there. Jerusalem, like Roma, is a city built on various hills, and the temple was on the one called Zion. It was an impressive structure, but not more magnificent than Roma's temples. Yet what went on in the Jerusalem temple was quite different from what happened in those."

Julia looked up, intensely interested. "What differences?"

"I'm getting to that," Prisca said patiently. "Just like Roman temples, this one had priests, sacrifices, various kinds of offerings, and a temple treasury where precious objects, important documents, and funds were kept."

Figure 2.4. Sappho, the famous poetess, was an educated woman.

Julia nodded.

"But in Herod's Temple non-Jews were only allowed in the outer courts, even if they were God-fearers like me. A stern warning on the entrance to the court of the Jews said that any Gentile crossing into that court could be killed on the spot!"

Julia looked surprised. She hadn't known about that.

Prisca wasn't looking at her, so she continued without comment. "There were also some synagogues not far from the temple; one on Mt. Ophel had an inscription in Greek which I could actually read! Priscilla was proud of me when I translated it into Latin for her, and we stayed in the hostel associated with this synagogue.

"The inscription on it read: 'Theodotus, son of Vettanos, a priest and a leader of the synagogue, son of a leader of the synagogue, and

Figure 2.5. Theodotus inscription.

grandson of a leader of the synagogue built the synagogue for the reading of Torah and for teaching the commandments; furthermore, the hostel, and the rooms, and the water installation for lodging needy strangers. Its foundation stone was laid by his ancestors, the elders, and Simonides.'

"But I've digressed a bit, which is allowed for elderly persons like me." Prisca smirked and Julia returned a smile. "Back to the temples, the differences are in some sense stark—no usual Roman festivals there, no images of deities, and the worship of only one God with absolutely no images of him. To those of us who grew up in non-Jewish environments this initially seemed strange, but at the same time it simplified and clarified religion, especially for me when I was young. If there really was only one God, it made perfect sense—and made religious life easier."

Julia couldn't keep still at hearing this. "Yes! The Roman religions are much too confusing with all their many capricious gods—"

Prisca held up her hand in protest. "If we get on that topic, we'll never finish this tale, Julia," she said with a laugh. Julia grinned and nodded as she lowered her head, ready to write again.

"On our first night there, Simon, the owner of the hostel, recounted to us visitors what had happened during the Passover festival fifty days prior. He explained that despite the fact it was festival season, three Jews had been crucified just before the Passover celebration proper had begun."

Julia nodded, knowing what Simon had been referring to.

"Jews reckon their days from sundown to sundown, unlike Romans, who reckon from dawn to dusk and dusk to dawn. And yet, those three men were still on crosses in the afternoon, with sundown coming shortly, on the day the lambs were sacrificed for the Passover feast. I could hardly believe it. This must have struck many Jews as such an inappropriate time for the governor to assert his authority to use capital punishment."

Prisca's voice quieted, so Julia looked up, only to see pain on her face. "Julia, I once saw a crucified man, gasping for breath beside the Appian Way.

He was having trouble breathing and writhing in pain. I could only imagine the horror of three persons crucified just outside the Holy City walls."

Both women grew still, and seconds went by as the image persisted in Prisca's mind until it became unbearable. She pulled her thoughts away from the memory, broke the silence, and continued her story.

"I sat and listened to Simon recount what happened. He was a vivid storyteller from the Diaspora, and his Greek was good. I later learned he attended the synagogue of the Hellenists, or Greek speakers, in Jerusalem.

"I can still see him clearly in the front room of that hostel on that night. Setting a large hand-lamp down next to him, the flame flickering, the shadows playing across his wrinkled face, Simon told a gruesome tale in a deep, resonant, compelling voice. It left such an impression on me, I can still remember his words:"

It was extraordinary. All three men had been nailed to crosses, and the centurions were there to make sure no one tried to rescue them. It seemed somehow appropriate that they were executed on a hill called Golgotha, the place of the skull. As we all know, crucifixion is not merely the most shameful way to die, called by the Romans "the extreme punishment" but it was a punishment reserved for the worst of the worst criminals—rebellious slaves, those who challenged the authority of Roman officials and so committed treason, and the like. We Jews also have a saying from Torah: "Cursed be he who hangs upon a tree." Some would say those men were surely cursed by God, and yet amazingly one was crucified with a placard that read, "Jesus of Nazareth, the King of the Jews." Imagine that—a crucified Jewish king. Unheard of, and the Scriptures do not foretell such a thing.[5]

"Simon cleared his throat and spat in a cup before he continued."

One malefactor died cursing God, another seems to have made his peace with God, but Jesus was the most extraordinary of all. He recited a psalm, and

---

[5]Early Jews before and during the era of Jesus did not read Isaiah 52–53 as a prophecy about a messiah. They read it as referring to the nation of Israel, who suffered for the sins of the world, for Israel is called "my servant" in the early portions of Isaiah 40–55.

then, amazingly; he forgave his executioners, praying something like "Abba, forgive them; they know not what they do." Incredible! But in the end, all three died and were hastily buried so as not to interfere either with Sabbath or Passover, both of which began at sundown. You would have thought that would be the end to that sad chapter in Jewish affairs in Jerusalem—but oh no!

"Simon paused and leaned forward, enjoying how his listeners did the same, waiting breathlessly for what would come next. When he was satisfied he had our rapt attention, he went on."

A mere day and a half later, the tomb where this Jesus had been laid was found empty. The tomb belonged to someone I know well—Joseph of Arimathea, a member of the Sanhedrin. He attended the same synagogue as some of my Aramaic-speaking fellow Jews. That tomb of his was empty!

"Simon wore a shocked look that we predictably reflected back to him."

Now, grave robbing is not unheard of, sadly, even in Jerusalem. Thieves won't even leave the dead alone in their hunt for possessions, mostly looking for coins and jewelry. But then we learned that Pilate had put a guard at the tomb at the request of the high priest Caiaphas. Grave robbing hardly seemed a likely explanation in those circumstances. And then, even more shockingly, some of Jesus' followers claimed they had seen him alive a few days after his crucifixion. I can tell you right now, we Jews were not looking for a crucified messiah, much less a crucified and risen one! And yet, that is what some Jews at the festival claimed—some from Galilee, but also some from here in Jerusalem.

Prisca added, "By this time, Simon really had my attention. I was hanging on his every word."

Old Cleopas told us he had personally walked with Jesus outside the city to Emmaus and had supped with him! Now, I'm as much a believer in the resurrection as any Pharisee, but Daniel didn't say there would be an isolated resurrection of a messiah one day. He spoke of a group resurrection of the righteous, and another group of the unrighteous.[6] And yet, the followers of

---

[6]Daniel 12:1-3.

Jesus have persisted and insisted that all this happened to Jesus, and that over forty days he appeared to a variety of people, and then, like Enoch or Elijah, ascended into heaven.

"Simon grew quieter now and looked thoughtful, almost forgetting his audience."

To me the most incredible part of this whole scenario is that people who saw Jesus die on the cross, and be buried, and by their own admission were not looking for his resurrection are the very people putting out this story that our God, blessed be he, had vindicated Jesus, and so made him a risen messiah. How can these things be? I believe in God's mighty works and healings as much as the next person. I've even run into a fellow named Eliezer, or Lazarus, just down the road in Bethany, who claims Jesus raised him from the dead, but Eliezer was not crucified, was not a criminal. This story is not merely shocking— it's a skandalon, as we say in Greek. It's just too much to swallow.

◆ ◆ ◆

Prisca smiled and swallowed a little wine. "What was it Jesus once said: What is impossible for human beings, is nonetheless possible for God? Yet I must confess, I found this story fascinating but beyond belief. Nothing I'd learned in the synagogue prepared me for this story, and it was at this juncture in Simon's tale that my mistress Priscilla said, 'That's more than enough bedtime stories for one night. We need to get some sleep. Tomorrow will be a big day in the festival and we want to get there early.'

"As I lay in bed that night, saying a prayer, I simply couldn't put that story out of my mind. I tossed and turned for some hours mulling it over, until I fell asleep, exhausted. Little did I know what the next day would hold for me and my mistress."

3

THE COST OF PENTECOST

Who knew the cost of Pentecost then or there,

Or the momentousness of the movement set in motion?

Who could have guessed the Guest who had inhabited them that day?

If possession is nine tenths of the law, then this magnificent possession

Became a magnificent obsession to lay down the Law and take up
the Gospel,

And so tip the world upside down such that peace came from grace
and truth,

Not law and order,

And testimony was borne not to a crime but to a crisis

Not to progress but to rescue,

Not to an Emperor, but to a Savior,

Not merely to the end of the old age,

But to the dawn of the new one.

As Prisca thought of those days, the years melted away and she was back in Jerusalem as a young girl. She remembered yawning and stretching as that new day dawned, the sun shining into the solitary window of their hostel room, her sense of anticipation making her restless until the *shophar,* the ram's horn, blew loud and clear from Mount Ophel, where they were staying.

The festival is about to begin! she thought with joy.

◆ ◆ ◆

Prisca snapped back to the present, once again aware that Julia was recording all of this. She straightened her garment and concentrated on what would be important for her daughter and future generations to know.

"The next morning we walked to the temple precincts where a large crowd had already gathered. To my astonishment, a group of people spoke to each of the language groups present in their own native tongues! They were talking about some sort of good news having to do with the very person Simon had been incredulous about—the crucified man from Nazareth, Jesus.

"Later I was to learn that God's Spirit had alighted on each one of these speakers and somehow had miraculously given them the ability to speak in other human languages. I have to admit when I learned that, I thought, *I'm sure this would horrify my Greek teacher, Herodes, back in Roma, because if this keeps happening, he'll be out of business!*"

Julia laughed out loud, loving the way Prisca could find humor in almost any situation.

"Then I remembered the story from the Torah about the tower in Babel, which I assume was the ancient name for Babylon, with its step-back temples. There the languages were confused or disseminated. Here the languages remained different, but some sort of miraculous good news overcame the language barrier. As I thought about this, someone in the crowd shouted, 'They must all be drunk! This is madness, and not appropriate at this celebration!'

"Just then a swarthy man of medium build with a considerable beard stood up and began to speak with a decided accent. Later I was to learn it was a Galilean accent, for this man was a fisherman from beside the sea of Tiberias in the northern part of the Promised Land.[1] Normally I might not pay much attention to yet another speech by an older man, but this man commanded our attention immediately. He had a presence, a spirit of sorts, and the crowd hushed when he began to speak."

Prisca paused and said, "Julia, as you know, exactly what Peter said is recorded near the beginning of Luke's second volume."[2]

Julia jumped up out of curiosity, anxious to read Peter's words again. So she went to the study, found the correct scroll, and unrolled it to the right spot.

Prisca listened quietly as Julia read Peter quoting the prophet Joel, and from the Psalms. When she finished, Prisca admitted, "To be honest, my memory is somewhat hazy, partly because of what was happening to and in me, and in my mistress as well. Like a fiery wind, God's Spirit seemed to fill me up, and I had a strange sense of warmth, of tingling, of excitement, of a compulsion to bow down and praise God. I looked across at my mistress and she was on her knees weeping, but hers were tears of joy. She had hoped to come and share in the joy of the festival, but she had not counted on encountering God so directly, so powerfully, and it brought her to her knees. I too, though I didn't understand the implications or cost of this experience at the time, was humbled by it all. I found myself speaking in a low voice, asking God to forgive my selfishness, my shortcomings, my immaturity. I had no idea what the ramifications of submitting to God really meant then.

---

[1]The sea of Galilee was called by several names including Kinneret, which means harp, perhaps because of the shape of the lake, but also it was called the sea of Tiberias by those from the western end of the empire (John 21:1).

[2]Acts 2:14-40.

Looking back now, I can say confidently, that was the day my life's journey took a completely different direction.

"Many of us were baptized that day in the name of the crucified and risen Jesus. And baptism became something valuable to me, so much so that later I had the courage to take aside a great church leader like Apollos and instruct him more accurately in the meaning of this baptism, which was similar to John the baptizer's baptism, but not the same in the end.

"This experience in Jerusalem led me to become part of what was originally called 'the Way' because Jesus himself was 'the Way' back to God.[3] I noticed that quite a few other people were praying in Latin, and on the return journey to Roma we traveled with several of them. We were all eager to share this good news about Jesus with our fellow Jews and God-fearers in the synagogue in Roma.[4] And that's how the good news finally reached the Eternal City; it was not from some mighty apostle, a Peter or a Paulus. It was not by a planned mission sent from what became the Jerusalem assembly of Jesus followers. No, we, the first converts to the Way, were like ordinary seeds thrown to the wind, blown to the west. And we were the first to plant that message from God in the Eternal City, and at no small cost.

"That cost became apparent immediately. Priscilla's husband was furious when he comprehended the message his wife had brought back with her from Jerusalem. He accused her of following a *superstitio,* a false religion. Within a week he gave her a decree of divorce, and we both moved out of our comfortable villa into a tenement in the *subura,* which Priscilla paid for with her dowry. She had enough money to provide for us for a while, but I knew I would need to find work, learn a trade, to help us survive."

---

[3] Acts 18:24-26.

[4] God fearers were not full proselytes to Judaism. They attended synagogue and embraced the one God and various laws of Moses. They did not go as far as circumcision, presumably partly because of the social stigma of a Gentile doing so, perhaps especially in Roma. Consider the tone of Juvenal who lampoons Judaism in his *Satires* (see the epigraph to the next chapter).

"Were you frightened?" Julia asked, imagining what it must have been like to be evicted from her comfortable home.

Prisca nodded. "Things were quite unsettled for a while. I wandered through the *subura* day after day from shop to shop, hoping for some work. I had some skill in sewing, so naturally I thought of the cloth merchants, but the guild of such merchants did not believe in hiring 'children,' as they called me, particularly females, though I was almost fifteen. But then God's favor shined on me, and I found work with the leather makers, who were desperately in need of hands to sew together tents, boots, and wineskins. Priscilla came as well, and we worked together as a team, earning our keep, enough to pay for our food, clothing, and necessities of life.

"These leather workers were partly from Roma and partly from abroad, and there was also a pious Jew from Pontus, on the northern sea above and east of Galatia. He was skilled in scraping and cutting the goat's hair cloth for various sizes of tents and other things made from animal skins. His name was Aquila, and he was a good five years older than me. At the time, it didn't occur to me that he would be anything other than a coworker. But some years later, as you well know, Aquila was to become my beloved husband."

Prisca paused and thought for a while, her chin relaxing from the weight of all the memories. Finally, she broke her reverie. "I think that's enough about the earliest part of my story. We'll pick this up again to tomorrow, Julia. Please remind me where we left off. I must remember to make clear that neither of the great apostles, Peter and Paulus, arrived in Roma before the reign of Nero. Indeed, in Paulus's case, he only arrived about four years before the great fire, and Peter only two. Even Apollos, who was to write that great sermon on faith and perseverance to the Jewish followers of Jesus in Roma after the fire, got there before the great apostles.[5] But I need to think more about the next part of the story, because it involved so much

---

[5] That is, Hebrews.

difficulty, including Aquila and me in exile when Claudius would brook no more disputes between Jews and Jewish followers of Jesus in Roma."

It was time to light the lamps in the house, for the winter sun disappeared more rapidly and earlier than in the summer months, and a chill had already crept into the house. Prisca summoned Achilles, her carpenter and tender of the home, to light the hearth fires. Winter was coming, and her woolen *stola* wouldn't be sufficient to keep Prisca from getting cold.

"You must eat something, Mistress, and drink some warm mulled wine as well," Julia offered. "Then we can say our prayers, asking for wisdom and strength for us both as you share your story."

"Yes," nodded Prisca. "It's easy to get absorbed in a task and forget the everyday necessities." Her face softened then, every line relaxing, making her look older and younger at the same time. "It's at this time of day I most miss my Aquila, even though he's been gone now for decades. He used to sing to me in the evenings and play the lyre, singing some of the Jewish songs, the *psalmoi*.[6] I miss that so much."

Prisca bowed her head, making Julia wish she could take all her mother's pain away. But a moment later, realizing she was succumbing to sentiment, Prisca straightened her back, stood, and her gentle smile returned. "Enough of that!" she said, putting an arm around Julia as they made their way down to dinner. "I still have you."

---

[6]She is referring to the Psalms, which were part of the liturgy of the temple and early Jewish worship. The Greek word *psalmos* means "song," whereas the Hebrew word *mizmor* means something closer to "melody of praise," or melody with instrumental accompaniment.

4

MAD CALIGULA, AND PERSISTENT AQUILA

Some who have had a father who reveres the Sabbath, worship nothing but the clouds, and the divinity of the heavens, and see no difference between eating swine's flesh, from which their father abstained, and that of man; and in time they take to circumcision. Having been wont to flout the laws of Roma, they learn and practice and revere the Jewish law, and all that Moses committed to his secret tome, forbidding to point out the way to any not worshipping the same rites, and conducting none but the circumcised to the desired fountain. For all which the father was to blame, who gave up every seventh day to idleness, keeping it apart from all the concerns of life.

JUVENAL, *SATIRE* 14

IT'S HARD TO LOOK BACK ON THE DECADE after the Master's crucifixion." Prisca absentmindedly wound the rag so tightly around her hand that Julia worried it would cut off her circulation.

Her mother had returned to her narrative after a hiatus of many weeks, while she'd mentally sifted various events from more than a half-century before. She'd been reluctant to return to the task at all, but this morning she sensed the first harbingers of spring and felt renewed enough to continue.

Julia waited as Prisca seemed to wrestle with an invisible foe. She wondered if the rag Prisca twisted represented her own tortured memories. Perhaps if she physically strangled them, she wouldn't have to face them now.

This had become a much slower process than Julia expected, and it worried her that Prisca wasn't sleeping as well since dredging up disturbing memories. The nightmares had increased rather than diminished. She hoped, for her mother's sake, that they were doing the right thing.

Finally, Prisca threw the rag onto the table and sat down. She sat erect and put her shoulders back, lifting her neck so that her chin was level. After taking a deep breath, she began once again. Julia sighed inwardly, admiring her mother's courage.

"So, where were we? Ah, yes. When Priscilla and I were cast out of our home, we lost our circle of pagan friends, but the Jews we knew in Roma didn't embrace us either. The vast majority of them thought the notion of a crucified and risen messiah was nonsense, and they claimed they couldn't find it in the Torah.

"So the few followers of Jesus in Roma soon found it difficult to meet with other Jews and God fearers in the synagogue in the *subura*. There was tension—and endless debates. Ordinarily, members of the synagogue enjoyed a good, heated dialogue, but these were not ordinary times, for Caligula had become the emperor after Tiberius, and he was repulsed by Jewish practice. Jews everywhere tried to keep a low profile, not cause trouble, not draw attention to themselves, and that included those who had returned from Jerusalem with a new faith in Jesus."

"Is that when the followers of the Christus began to meet separately, outside the synagogue?"

"Yes, and when they did attend the synagogue, they didn't engage in dialogue or debate about Jesus, so the shalom of the Sabbath wouldn't be broken. Still, the tensions rose to the surface from time to time.

"But I'm getting ahead of myself. I must give you some background to help you understand why most of Roma hated the Jews, who were the butt of many slurs, slanders, and jokes such as those later used by Juvenal.[1]

"When I was born, Tiberius was still emperor. At that time the laws and rules Octavian—or as he preferred, 'Augustus'—had set up were still enforced, including laws about religions. So Jews were allowed to practice their religion and didn't have to worship the emperor, only offer sacrifices and prayers on his behalf. But Romans in general disliked Jews, calling them *atheoi*—that is, atheists—because they refused to worship the traditional Greek and Roman gods.

"But Augustus also set up laws against eastern religious cults in an attempt to revive traditional moral and religious values. To that end he made both stricter marriage and adultery laws, and spent time and money on repairing or rebuilding temples of the traditional gods. He particularly despised some of the 'new' eastern religions that had come along with foreigners to Roma— for example, the cult of Isis from Egypt. Patrician women were not to participate in such religions as it was considered 'unRoman.'"

Prisca sighed and picked up the rag once more. "It was a confusing time for followers of Christus. If the officials determined we were not really Jews, we could fall under the laws banning various eastern cults or, worse, be forced to offer a libation and other forms of worship to the emperor, especially if, as like myself, we were gentile in origin but Jewish in religious orientation."

"What happened when Caligula took the throne? Did things get better?"

Prisca vigorously shook her head. "Caligula rose to the throne some seven years after the crucifixion of Jesus, and he was truly mad. He was the first

---

[1] Juvenal wrote during the time Prisca's narrative was composed, in the AD 90s.

emperor to believe he was a god, and he insisted his subjects worship him. He despised anyone who suggested there was only one god *and that it wasn't him.* He attempted to put his own statue in the Jerusalem temple.

"For the first couple of years, Caligula's real nature and predilections didn't come to light. But Philo of Alexandria and Seneca the Stoic philosopher described Caligula as an insane emperor who was narcissistic, killed on a whim, spent wildly, and was addicted to sex.[2] But this wasn't all. The government was in a financial crisis, made worse by a famine in Egypt, the breadbasket of the empire. Even Caligula realized he couldn't simply stop the dole without riots in Roma, but he curtailed it, tried to limit it to only poor Roman citizens, eliminating foreigners, slaves, and others. But this action proved too much and was one of things that led to his assassination eleven years after Jesus died."

Prisca sighed and shook her head to rid her mind of the despicable man. Speaking of Caligula seemed to drain her of energy and vitality. But after a few moments, she once again put the rag down and found the courage that always seemed to come to her when she most needed it. Her voice grew stronger, her concentration having returned to what came next in her story.

"Enough about that. Back to Priscilla and me. We made do with a more modest lifestyle and worked hard at the leather-worker's shop in the *subura.* We were required to join the tentmakers' guild, called the *collegium tabernaculariorum,* and Aquila was the one to help us understand how important this was. He said, 'Being a member of the guild gives us something of a safety net, for the guild members look after each other when there is illness or misfortune, and they pay for the burial rites as well.'

"The guild was wealthy enough to buy and maintain its own building, called a *schola,* where we had regular meetings. C. Iulius Chrysantius, the

---

[2]Seneca the Younger, *On Anger* xviii.1, *On Anger* III.xviii.1; *On the Shortness of Life* xviii.5; Philo of Alexandria, *On the Embassy to Gaius* XXIX.

guild's most notable member, was a freedman of Augustus, and so was quite old when we got to know him. He was the *aedituus*[3] of our *schola*.[4]

"I enjoyed the sewing work, and as time went on, Aquila began to talk to Priscilla about my being betrothed to him. I didn't object to this, not least because it would relieve Priscilla of some of her financial burdens. But at the same time I was fearful, because so far as I could tell, Aquila was not a follower of the Christus. He was a Jew and never worked on the Sabbath, arranging with Chrysantius to work extra on other days.

"During all this turmoil, I kept working, remained quiet, didn't make waves or trouble for anyone, but I kept my faith in Jesus and prayed faithfully, as Aquila kept talking to me and to Priscilla about marrying me. Finally, I could keep my faith a secret no longer. Priscilla encouraged me to have a frank conversation with Aquila about this matter."

Prisca couldn't help grinning. "You know, Julia, God is full of surprises. All along, I assumed Aquila was just an ordinary Jew. I was wrong. Very wrong. Full of fear, I said, 'I believe you are a trustworthy man and must ask you to keep what I am about to tell you in confidence.'

"Aquila smiled and said, 'Well that's a relief. I'm glad you don't think I'm a wolf in sheep's clothing. Actually, he spoke to me in Latin, not Greek, and said, '*Pelle sub agnina latitat mens saepe lupine.*'[5] The Master, Jesus himself, used this analogy,[6] so Aquila was actually paraphrasing Jesus! Even more amazing, Aquila was in Jerusalem at Pentecost with friends from Pontus[7] and was converted to faith in Christus at the same time I was! Unlike me, he stayed in Jerusalem for some months after Pentecost to learn the teachings of Jesus from Peter and Jacob and others. God really does work all things together for good!

---

[3]The word means guardian.
[4]There is inscriptional evidence about all this, including Chrysantius, who was a real person. See CIL 6.5183B, 6.9053 and 9053a.
[5]An old Roman proverb that means "Under a sheep's skin hides a wolf-like mind."
[6]Matthew 7:15.
[7]Acts 2:10.

"When Aquila told me this, I was overcome, and burst into tears." Prisca took the rag, twisted beyond recognition by now, and dabbed at her eyes. "Even now, it brings me to tears. I was so relieved, so thankful that I simply blurted out, 'Then God himself must have been charting our courses so we would meet one day and marry.' Aquila just laughed and said, 'Well then, we should get on with it. Don't want to be hindering the work of God himself!'"

Prisca laughed at the memory and Julia blushed, flooded with warmth to hear it. "As it turned out, Aquila had been meeting secretly with other Jewish followers of Jesus at the house of a well-to-do widow, Miriam. We were married the very year that Caligula was assassinated and shy, reluctant Claudius ascended to the throne. And despite all the political turmoil, we were very happy. I moved into Aquila's apartment in the *insula,* which was in the *subura,* and we began, with Priscilla's blessing, to make a home and try to have a family."

At this point, Prisca put the rag to her eyes once more, but quickly removed it, ashamed for weeping like an old woman. Julia wanted to reassure her that her tears were all right, but Prisca quickly went on. "After some years of trying, it became evident that I was not able to have children, and Aquila took this very hard at first. He prayed and prayed for God to open my womb, but . . . it never happened. We were otherwise happy and well matched, though he was my elder by a good five years, and we had little vision for what might come next."

Prisca fell silent, so Julia asked, "Was Claudius a better ruler?"

"Well, he was certainly less unpredictable than Caligula, but he was very traditional like Augustus and had no patience with quarreling foreigners, especially Jews. Sometimes life is what happens to you when you are making other plans, and so Aquila and I found ourselves exiled from Roma!"

Achilles stood in the doorway and Prisca broke off abruptly and said, "*Tempus fugit*—it's past our dinner time!"

Julia felt Prisca had left her hanging at a particularly interesting part of the tale, but she could see the fatigue on Prisca's face, so she took her by the hand and led her into the *triclinium*, where they regularly dined. She called Clemens, who was sitting in the peristyle garden, and they sat down to a meal of bread with *garum* (the fish pickle relish so beloved by Romans), some broth, a cup of wine laced with honey, and some olives and dates. Prisca's diet did not include much meat, as her old stomach couldn't take it anymore. Julia looked around the room with satisfaction as they said the traditional Jewish blessing: "Blessed are you Adonai our God who brings forth bread from the earth . . . "

Figure 4.1. The *triclinium* served as a dining room. People reclined on the couches while reaching for food and wine on the small, central table.

5

A MARRIAGE ARRANGED IN ROMA

*Are you, in this day and age, ready for an agreement, a contract, the
wedding vows, having your hair done by a master-barber, your finger
already wearing the pledge? Postumus, you were sane once. Are you
really taking a wife? Which Tisiphone is it, with her snakes, driving
you mad? You surely don't have to endure it, with so much rope about
those vertiginous windows open, the Aemilian bridge at hand?*

JUVENAL, *SATIRE* 6.25-27

JULIA WALKED INTO THE ROOM just as Clemens left. Prisca paced
the floor, more energetic and excited than she had been over anything
in months.

"Can you believe it, Julia? All our long years of making tents, boots,
sandals, gladiator's attire, and now this? My shop is supposed to pour all its
energies and efforts into making awnings for the Coliseum—and not just
any kind of awnings. Awnings that will shade the whole outer perimeter,
the whole outer third of the audience? And they want it in red! The Emperor

Domitianus insists! And furthermore, there's now a new office of management set up by the emperor called *Praepositus valeris castrensibus*—the office to oversee the making of *valerii*—awnings! Romans are capable of over-organizing and creating more bureaucracy for anything.

"First the cry was 'Bread and circuses, bread and circuses' to keep the masses content and not thinking of revolution. Now, the games are more important than the army, and the gladiators more important than senators. Where is this all going to end? Men and their games!"

"*Domina*, calm yourself." Julia ran to Prisca's side and gently took her arm. "Stop pacing the floor. At least it's business. At least you will keep your freedmen and women employed. *Why not* become more prosperous at Domitianus's expense?"

Prisca looked annoyed. "Roma's rulers and ruling class seem more concerned with their own entertainment than its health, prosperity, and safety. It's a distraction from the real issues of life."

Julia decided it best to change the subject. "Speaking of life's issues, we broke off our narrative after you got married, while Claudius was about to be made emperor. Shall we pick up the story there?"

Prisca, flushed in the face and still pacing, took a few minutes to calm down. They decided to sit in the peristyle garden as the spring air was delicious. Prisca noticed the shadow on the sundial[1] and took in the beauty of the flower beds and bushes—oleander, acanthus, narcissus, violets, irises, and a beautiful purple bougainvillea vine hanging from a trellis over one of the seats. But in spite of the garden's pleasures, Prisca couldn't let her angst go.

---

[1] The problem, of course, with sundials is that there is less sun in the winter than in the summer, so in effect, in winter, hours are forty-five minutes long if you are dividing the day from dawn to dusk into twelve increments, but at the height of the summer the hours are seventy-five minutes long. See Angelo Angela, *A Day in the Life of Ancient Rome* (New York: Europa Editions, 2009), 75.

"This is all Chrysantius's fault. He's the one who bought a wooden amphitheater then realized it would be too hot in the summer since it was located on Mars Field." She sat down only to stand and pace once more. "And then Nero bought the place from Chrysantius and had him install awnings over it so he wouldn't sweat too much when he recited his poetry there or played his lyre to 'captive' audiences." She added with a smirk, "Captive, because his household was mostly slaves, and so literally captives."

This wry thought helped her relax enough to sit down again. "He even had the undersides of the awnings painted with blue stars to simulate the night sky. Nero got the idea from Julius Caesar, who had already erected such awnings over the Forum in the center of the city because of all the heat coming off the marble tiles, temples, and the like."[2]

Warming to her thoughts and to the fair sunlight of the garden, she went on. "The original awnings were actually made of linen, and so lightweight, but we tentmakers were used to adapting. The result of the little deal between Nero and Chrysantius was that he became—I can hear the herald blowing his horn now—'Imperial Tentmaker Supreme,' which meant that the emperor always got his orders made first.

"Chrysantius was nothing if not resourceful. Soon we began to have little tent-coverings for cisterns to keep the water cooler, tent coverings or awnings over peristyle gardens[3] to shade them from the sun. They were colored red, the same red often used on the painted inside walls of houses. People wanted awnings or small tents for picnic outings, weddings, and such. It was all the fashion."

Suddenly the emotional storm was over as soon as it had started. "Speaking of weddings, let's carry on with our story." ·

"At last!" Julia agreed with a teasing smile.

---

[2]See Suetonius, *Caesar* 39 on this, and also Pliny, *Natural History* 19.23.
[3]The atrium was the garden.

Prisca returned the smile broadly and gave Julia a hug. "I'm sorry. It feels like one thing after another sometimes. I just needed to let off some steam."

Julia returned the embrace. "I understand. You've been through so much. My life has been easy in comparison, thanks to you. I'll gladly listen to your rants anytime."

"Well, let's back up. I want to tell you more about my wedding."

Julia nodded and picked up her stylus.

"Since I was a Roman citizen, and Aquila was of lower social status in the eyes of the world, we had a Roman wedding, with some Christian modifications. We did not share the jaundiced view of marriage that Juvenal, our resident satirist, did. I'm sometimes asked why my name is regularly put first when we are both mentioned, but it should be obvious it's because of the social status issue, not because Aquila was somehow a nonentity.[4] But what did it matter? We were one in Christus and equal in the eyes of God.

"As you know, the word *matrimonium* means taking a woman to be not merely a wife but a *mater*, a mother. Romans see having children who can be legitimate heirs and perpetuate the family's good name as the purpose of marriage. While it was normal practice to require the consent of both the father of the bride and of the groom, in our case, we were far removed from our fathers in space and in time. In fact, I wasn't even sure who my father was. So, our marriage was odd in that it was not an arranged marriage, but this often happened."

Prisca studied Julia for a moment. "Even though the legal age for marriage is twelve for girls and fourteen for boys, that's far too young. Thankfully, most girls marry in their late teens. In the early decades of the empire the legal status of girls was little different than boys, in part because so many women died in childbirth, and so there was a great need for women to get married."

---

[4] Romans 16:3 and Acts 18:26.

She paused, so Julia took the opportunity to clarify something she'd been wondering. "You kept your mistress's name at marriage because in Roman law a daughter retains her given or birth-family name, since a Roman citizen's daughter can inherit. I've heard in some other cultures, women aren't allowed to inherit?"

"That's true. Roma has been fair in that regard. I may become frustrated with our leaders, but they have done some things well."

Bemused by this thought, Prisca waited a moment before she continued. "The form of wedding we had was *confarreatio,* the more patrician form of wedding, which involved the ceremonial sharing of spelt bread. For this we substituted the Lord's Supper. It seemed only appropriate, though some of our guests were puzzled by the substitution. Ours was what was called a 'free marriage,' a marriage of equals, despite the inequities of social status and rank. As you pointed out, Roman women have a degree of independence not found in various cultures in the eastern part of the empire, and I've come to appreciate that as time has worn on. I've seen many women in arranged marriages who were either abused, beaten, unloved, or profoundly unhappy."

Julia shuddered. She often longed for marriage, but this was a good reminder that she was wise in her patience.

"Normally the *Flamen Dialis,* or high priest of Jupiter, and perhaps another high priest would need to be present at a *confarreatio* wedding, but we didn't have a normal pagan wedding. We improvised, and a Jewish friend of Aquila's bore witness at our wedding."

"Tell me about your wedding dress!" Julia knew that a Roman bride usually made her own wedding dress, which would have been no problem for Prisca, considering her profession. Most people, however, had to use an older dress and repurpose it. That sort of dress would be taken to the *fullonica,*[5] where it would first be soaked in a mixture of water and urine,

---

[5] The laundry.

then dried, and then bleached by hanging it over a foul-smelling sulfur brazier. That produced the whitest garments possible, but they needed to be aired out for a good period of time to lose the smell.[6] "I mean, I know the nasty-smelling process it takes to make the dress," Julia said, "but what was your dress like?"

"I wore a traditional white woolen dress with a yellow veil. I liked that it symbolized purity and chastity before marriage. As you know, virginity is of utmost importance for a bride, which is perhaps one reason girls marry so young. Also, as was customary, we exchanged gifts before the wedding ceremony, and Aquila gave me this ring with a beautiful lapis lazuli stone in it from Egypt."

She held out her hand to admire once more her prized possession, which never left her finger.

"The night before the wedding, the bride gives away her childhood playthings and clothes, laying them on the altar of the *Lares,* or household deity. Instead, I gave them to our Christian assembly's clothing room for the poor. I donned my dress and a veil with a floral wreath on my head, and a torchbearer led our joyful process from Priscilla's to Aquila's house. Once at Aquila's doorstep, I was given water and fire, symbols that I must attend the chores of keeping the home fires burning and the house clean. I was carried over the threshold by my two bridesmaids, who were friends from work, at which point the sacred vows were said: '*ubi tu Gaius, ego Gaia.*' Only we substituted our own names—'Where you are Aquila, I am Prisca,' and he said the reverse. We then clasped right hands, and the marriage ceremony ended. Aquila's Jewish friend offered a benediction of 'The LORD bless you and keep you; the LORD make his face shine on you and be gracious to you; the LORD turn his face toward you and give you peace. Amen.'"[7]

---

[6]Angela, *A Day in the Life,* 76-77.
[7]Numbers 6:24-26.

Prisca chuckled. "Some of the guests were confused by this and thought he was referring to the blessing of the Lord of Roma, namely the emperor. I must confess I giggled when I heard that suggestion after the ceremony."

Prisca put a hand to her mouth and kept sniggering. Julia loved to see her laugh.

"Oh, where was I? We consummated our marriage in complete darkness, and the next day we had a dinner party for all ten guests. Priscilla paid for the wedding, and also gave me a small dowry, which by tradition was given directly to Aquila for safekeeping. Aquila never spent it, which turned out to be fortunate for me."

Julia interrupted. "Domina, were you happy? Was it a good love match?"

"Oh yes, from the very outset. For the first couple of years, we were completely happy, but then came the day when Aquila had an argument about Christus in the synagogue in the *subura*. But we should save the next chapter of this story for another day, and instead enjoy the memories of that wedding day for now."

Julia was quiet, and then in an exasperated tone said, "Domina, I despair of ever finding such a husband—a good follower of Christus."

Prisca knew this sorrow of Julia's. Now in her thirties, she had little chance of finding a suitable husband. She leaned forward and placed a hand on Julia's knee. "You know I've always wanted this for you. Don't give up hope."

"Thank you. I've accepted that it's unlikely, but it's nice to know you haven't given up the possibility for me."

Prisca thought back to being a young woman with only Priscilla to love her. What would she have done without Aquila? "Priscilla died shortly after the joy of the wedding. They placed her ashes in a jar in the Priscillan catacomb in the *columbarium* with the inscription: 'For Junia Priscilla, a loving friend and good mother to Prisca, who survived many misfortunes with good humor, through the help of her Lord Christus. Known for her unflinching loyalty and self-sacrificial love to all, she rests in peace within

Figure 5.1. A pathway through the Priscillan catacomb. Notice the burial niches in the walls.

this place.'"[8] *I'm thankful she lived long enough to see me happily married, and she passed into the afterlife just before Aquila and I were sent into exile,* Prisca thought, but did not express aloud. *That horror, I'm glad she did not live to see.*

And, as one part of Prisca's life ended, another began.

---

[8]The Priscillan catacomb really exists, and scholars have for many years speculated about whether it was connected to the Biblical Priscilla. In any case, it is named after a high-status Roman woman.

6

BANISHED!

Since the Jews constantly made disturbances at the instigation of Chrestus, he [the Emperor Claudius] expelled them from Rome.

SUETONIUS, *DIVUS CLAUDIUS* 25

Instead of the social mobility that modern historiography makes so much of . . . the true mobility of the Roman craftsman was often geographical.

J. P. MOREL, IN *THE ROMANS*

PRISCA CONTINUED HER STORY WITH JULIA: "It's hard for me to tell this part of the story, Julia . . . indeed, very hard. There was an argument in the synagogue that led to a fight. Aquila tried to break it up, putting him in the middle of it. One of the higher-status Jews reported the situation to the nearby *vigilis* station in the *subura,* who in turn passed the news on to the officials in Caesar's household, and before long there was a decree. We had exactly one week to pack up everything and not merely get out of Roma but get out of all Italia, only to return when Claudius no

---

Quotation from J. P. Morel: "The Craftsman," in *The Romans,* A. Giardina, ed. (University of Chicago Press, 1993), 233.

longer ruled. It came as an utter shock, as Aquila had not been the instigator of the fight though he had bruises from it. There was no trial, just a decree, and even I as a Roman citizen was not allowed to protest, for my husband was a Jew, and Claudius would brook no due process for troublesome Jews.

"Suddenly, we had to pack things in crates and hire passage on a boat from Ostia, but where would we go? Aquila knew a few people in the guild who had spent time in Corinth and said it was a safe place for us to get away from our troubles. And so, to the Roman colony city of Corinth we went. Our friends at work were shocked, and sympathetic, but they could do nothing. Fortunately, Priscilla had passed away quietly and did not live to see this sorry day."

Figure 6.1. The *Milliarium aureum,* or golden milestone, from which "all roads lead."

"It must have been awful for you, since you'd already had to leave home once. And with you so newly married!"

"Yes, it was. I hadn't realized how much my sense of security and safety was tied up in having a home and decent job. With those things suddenly ripped away, I felt lost. I knew my hope was to be in Jesus and not in my circumstances, but it took a good deal of time for me to feel settled and safe again after this crisis. They say that 'all roads lead to Roma,' and indeed the roads of the empire do, but we were going in the opposite direction, and it did not augur well in my Roman soul."[1]

---

[1]There was in the Forum in the center of Rome the *Milarium Aureum* or Golden Milestone built in 20 BC, from which all distances from Rome were measured, and many of them were carved

Julia asked, "What was Corinth like?"

"Corinth had a long and checkered history. After a quiet period in the early second century before Christus,[2] Roman General Mummius utterly destroyed the city, except for the famous ancient temple of Apollo in the center of the old city, but it was then rebuilt under the auspices of Julius Caesar. So it felt newer than Roma. Since it was a Roman colony city, Roman soldiers held sway and the system of Roman jurisprudence was the law of the city, which made it feel much like Roma in that way. During this same period, Corinth eclipsed Athens in economic prowess, with seaports in both directions, east and west, and was named the province of Achaia's capital, much to the Athenians' annoyance," Prisca added with a crooked smile. "By the time we got there it had a population of some fifty thousand and had become the largest slave market and trading center outside of Roma and Alexandria.[3]

"When we arrived in Corinth, weary and laden down with our belongings, we had no idea where we would live. Our goods had to be hauled up the *diolkos* by an ox cart and then on to the city."

"I can't imagine that," Julia said, looking up from her writing. "It must have been terrifying."

"Not terrifying as much as exhausting and overwhelming. Aquila left me to travel with the cart as he hurried ahead to find the guild of cloth- and tentmakers' offices in the city, where he hoped to get advice as to where we could live and practice our trade.

"Fortuna, or better said, God's providence, was with us, because the Isthmian games had become so popular that there was a desperate need for more tentmakers and cloth sewers in Corinth. The games were held every

---

into the bronze surface of the milestone. See Angelo Angela, *A Day in the Life of Ancient Rome* (New York: Europa Editions, 2009), 206.

[2]The quote above describes the situation in about 196 BC. The Isthmian games were held just outside of Corinth, near the Isthmus, hence the name.

[3]See Ben Witherington III, *Conflict and Community in Corinth* (Grand Rapids: Eerdmans, 1996).

Figure 6.2. Small boats were dragged on carts across the *diolkos* to avoid a longer water journey.

two years, and it looked like we would have steady work if we could just get along with our fellow guild members. Aquila was a naturally outgoing person with a winning personality, and he soon impressed Ajax, the head of the guild in Corinth.

"As it turned out, there was a whole tenement block where cloth workers lived, a sort of mini-*subura* in the ancient city."

Prisca stood to take a piece of fruit from a bowl, ruining the attractive arrangement. Julia asked, "Did you find it hard to adjust?"

Prisca turned to her and thought a moment. "Yes, Roman citizens made up the elite and ran most of the city, but they were the minority. Most everyone spoke Greek, not Latin, so we had to become much more proficient in Greek, which took some time. Also, Corinth seemed small compared to Roma, but I liked being near two different seas—the Adriatic and the Aegean, the famous wine-dark seas of Homer."

Julia remembered something she'd overheard. "Domina, Corinth had the reputation of being a morally corrupt place, even in ancient Greek times

before the empire. There was a saying 'not for every man was the journey to Corinth.'[4] Is this judgment fair?"

Prisca pursed her lips and dropped her head. "From a Jewish or Christus follower point of view, Corinth was a considerable moral challenge. Many transients came through Corinth, and the slave trade brought a lot of unsavory people. Industry from both ports led to many brothels. It's no wonder Paulus spent over a year and a half in Corinth trying to make sure the faith of Jesus was well rooted in its rocky soil."

Figure 6.3. The ancient temple of Apollo. The hill above is the acropolis, where the temple of Aphrodite was located.

She became lost in her thoughts as Julia faithfully wrote. After a time, she realized Julia was waiting for her to continue. "I keep getting sidetracked. That's a story for another day because we lived in Corinth almost a decade before Paulus showed up, and there were some followers of Jesus, like us, already in the city.

"Back to our story. When Aquila and I first arrived in Corinth, we had to start at the bottom. We had to take what work we could and make sure

---

[4]Julia is quoting from Horace, *Epistles* 1.17.36; cf. also Strabo, *Geography* 8.6.20. Quintus Horatius Flaccus, or Horace, lived during the time of Julius Caesar in the first century BC, and his letters were famous. Some of his aphorisms, however, were so famous, like this one, that one need not have read his letters to know it.

we did the highest-quality work possible so we would continue to get more work. It was a big struggle. Actually, I was thankful at the time that we had neither children nor servants, because we lived hand to mouth for many months and barely had enough for ourselves. We'd saved some *denarii*[5] in Roma, but we exhausted our savings within the first year or two, trying to survive. However, Aquila refused to touch my dowry, which I objected to at the time but was thankful for later."

Prisca fell silent, seeming to be stuck in that difficult period. Julia shifted in her seat, trying to get a crick out of her neck, and decided to prod her on. "Will you tell me about religious life in Corinth?"

Figure 6.4. These silver denarii feature Nero, who succeeded Claudius in AD 54.

Prisca perked up at this subject. "Oh, yes. There was a considerable Jewish community in Corinth; several hundred people were either ethnic Jews or God fearers or proselytes. You could visit their synagogue today, were we there.

"At first we were well received in the synagogue. Irenic, friendly Stephanus was the synagogue leader. Paulus later led him and his family to faith in the Lord and baptized them.[6] But more important during our early days in Corinth, we came to know Titius Justus, who like me was a Roman who had become a God fearer and then a follower of Jesus.[7] He, more than anyone, truly embraced us and helped us make the transition to Corinth.

"Titius also had been exiled from Roma by Claudius's edict. His Roman citizen status helped him get a foothold in Corinth. I began to realize the Lord was developing a network of believers all across the empire, a family of faith that believers could turn to for fellowship and brotherly help."

---

[5] The silver denarius was perhaps the most important of the Roman coins for transacting business. It was about the size of a dime, and of course had a picture of the current or recent emperor on it.

[6] 1 Corinthians 1:16.

[7] Acts 18:7.

Figure 6.5. The lintel of the synagogue in Corinth. It shows part of the inscription "synagoge Hebraoi."

Julia was delighted to finally get details about this mysterious time in Prisca's life. "What was your role among the Christus followers there?"

Prisca's answer was firm. "Neither Aquila nor I had the gift of evangelism, but as time went on, we found we were gifted in teaching and instructing disciples, such as Titius Justus and Sosthenes the scribe.[8] We continued to go to the synagogue and make friends, but we didn't interrupt the service and bear witness there. We decided on quiet diplomacy outside the synagogue, not wishing to be cast out of a second city under Roman law. Mostly, we worked hard and saved our *denarii,* looking forward to the day when we could go home.

"It was in Titius's home that we got news about what was happening in Jerusalem, for he often opened his home to wayfarers. We heard about Stephen's death, the first person 'in Christus' to be martyred, and then the death of Jacob son of Zebedee at the hands of Herod Agrippa, only a few years after we arrived in Corinth.[9] We heard about deliberate persecutions in connection with Stephen, an intentional effort by the Jewish authorities

---

[8]1 Corinthians 1:1.

[9]See Acts 7 on Stephen and Acts 12:1-2 on Jacob. All the so-called Jameses in the New Testament are really Jacobs, named after the patriarch. The name James comes from translation of *Jacobus* into European languages and eventually into English.

against our movement, and in particular we heard about one zealous Pharisee named Saul of Tarsus, who, not long before we had to move to Corinth, converted to faith in Jesus. It happened through some miraculous experience when he was on his way to Damascus to extradite more followers of Jesus and take them to Jerusalem for trial. We thanked God for that divine intervention, which mostly stopped the persecutions by Jesus' own people, but we could've never imagined what would come next."

Prisca stopped suddenly, clearly lost in thought. But Julia couldn't stand to leave it there. "Well?"

"Hm?" Her mother seemed lost in thought.

"What happened next?" she asked.

"Oh, forgive me." Prisca smiled. "After we had been in Corinth for almost a decade without incident, a small man with a prominent forehead, a beard, a crooked nose and bowed legs said, 'Greetings in the name of the Lord, my name is Paulus,' and on that day our lives would change course once more, in a completely unexpected direction."[10]

---

[10] *The Acts of Paul and Thecla,* 2.3: "And he saw Paul coming, a man little of stature, thin-haired upon the head, crooked in the legs, of good state of body, with eyebrows joining, and nose somewhat hooked, full of grace: for sometimes he appeared like a man, and sometimes he had the face of an angel." This comes from the late second century, and Tertullian tells us it was written not long before his time, to honor Paul.

7

PAULUS THE APOSTLE IN CORINTH

After this, Paul left Athens and went to Corinth. There he met a Jew named Aquila, a native of Pontus, who had recently come from Italy with his wife Priscilla, because Claudius had ordered all Jews to leave Rome. Paul went to see them, and because he was a tentmaker as they were, he stayed and worked with them. Every Sabbath he reasoned in the synagogue, trying to persuade Jews and Greeks.

ACTS 18:1-4

What pleasure can it give you, Tucca, to mix with old Falernian wine new wine stored up in Vatican casks? What vast amount of good has the most worthless of wine done you? or what amount of evil has the best wine done you? As for us, it is a small matter; but to murder Falernian, and to put poisonous wine in a Campanian cask, is an atrocity. Your guests may possibly have deserved to perish: a wine-jar of such value has not deserved to die.

MARTIAL, *EPIGRAMS* 1.18

Quotations from Martial: Martial was the wit of choice in the last third of the first century (AD 41-102, approximately). His epigrams were widely quoted in the last decade of the first century, the time period when Prisca's chronicle is also being composed.

You imagine yourself Caecilius, a man of wit. You are no such thing, believe me. What then? A low buffoon; such a thing as wanders about in the quarters beyond the Tiber, and barters pale-colored sulphur matches for broken glass; such a one as sells boiled peas and beans to the idle crowd; such as a lord and keeper of snakes; or as a common servant of the salt-meat-sellers; or a hoarse-voiced cook who carries round smoking sausages in steaming shops.

MARTIAL, *EPIGRAMS* 1.41

WHATEVER ELSE ONE NEEDS TO SAY about Paulus, for such was his Latin name, he was a remarkable man in many respects, and no one I've ever met could match his zeal for the Lord, his intensity, his sheer energy," Prisca continued. Prisca was pacing her garden once more, and Julia struggled to write while following her matron around. She could tell that Prisca saw this as a crucial juncture in her own life and in the lives of Christus's followers.

"Aquila and I never imagined we'd meet an apostle. Of course, I'd heard Peter preach when I was fourteen and visited Jerusalem, but I never met him.

"By the way, as I mentioned, there were already Christus followers in Corinth before Paulus ever showed up, so I'm always concerned with reports that the apostles went around founding our assemblies across the empire. I bring this up because, if I'm going to be an advocate of truth, I need to be honest about what actually happened. But it took the apostles and their gifts of evangelism to turn what was at best a minority mission into a real movement that one official was later to say 'turned the world upside down.'[1] Humanly speaking, it couldn't have been accomplished without these gifted apostles."

---

[1] Acts 17:6.

To Julia's relief, Prisca calmed herself enough to sit. Her voice slowed, her eyes glinting as she remembered a long-ago time, place, and person.

"And yet . . . Paulus was not an amazing orator, though he knew the art of persuasion. While his speaking voice was strong enough, he had what the rhetoricians call an *ethos* problem—that is, his physical appearance and presentation distracted his listeners."

This surprised Julia. "Did he wear a silly looking toga, or a hair piece, or use stilted gestures or manners, like some rhetoricians?"

Prisca laughed, "Thankfully, no." Then she grew more sober. "Paulus had experienced eye problems ever since his vision of Jesus on Damascus Road. Yes, he could see, but his eyes kept watering and oozing some kind of discharge, which is why he says in his letter to those in Galatia that they would have plucked out their eyes and given them to him if they could.[2]

"This was an ongoing problem for Paulus on many counts. For one thing, some questioned how he could be a true prophet or seer if he couldn't *see* clearly. We all considered the eyes the windows of the soul, and so, if one had weak or problematic eyes, what did that tell a person who judged by appearances about Paulus's soul? Paulus called this his 'thorn in the flesh from Satan,'[3] and that's why he frequently had to rely on people like you, Julia."

Julia sat a little straighter. "Like me? How so?"

"He had to rely on *amaneuenses*, or scribes, such as Sosthenes in Corinth, or later Tertius when he wrote to the Romans, since his eyes made writing difficult, though normally he would sign his letters at the end with a personal message in large letters.[4] He told us that God allowed this painful condition to keep him humble and reliant on the Lord every single day. And that was the most notable feature about the man—his constant communion with and reliance on the Lord—and why people listened to him in spite of his ailment."

---

[2]Galatians 4:14-16.
[3]2 Corinthians 12:7-9.
[4]Galatians 6:11; 2 Thessalonians 3:17.

Prisca wore a pensive expression as she reflected on this. "And yet . . . there were people who, when they looked at Paulus closely, were afraid he might cast an evil eye and curse them. Paulus records in his letter to the Galatians that he was surprised they did not spit to ward off the curse when they saw his affliction but instead received him as an angel from God because of his divine message."[5]

At that moment, Clemens entered the garden to ask Prisca a question about a patron who wanted a special order. Prisca dealt with it quickly and efficiently.

"Now where were we . . . Oh! When we came to know Paulus, he was already beginning to travel with a physician named Luke, who ministered to his condition from things he had learned from Hippocrates.[6]

"When Paulus first visited us in Corinth, he didn't know we were followers of Christus; he was simply looking for work in Corinth, for he too was a tentmaker. He and his family had long practiced this trade in Tarsus, where they made tents out of goat's hair skin or cloth. In fact, as Paulus was later to relate, this is how he and his family came to be granted Roman citizenship—for services to the Empire, namely making tents for the legions that were stationed in or passed through Tarsus in the province of Cilicia and Syria."

"Why didn't Paulus ask for patronage as was his due as a minster of the Lord?" Julia asked.

"From the outset, Paulus wanted to offer the good news free of charge in Corinth, as he also needed to be free to travel. That said, he didn't have a problem with receiving funds from converts, because he did in Philippi. Indeed,

---

[5]Galatians 4:14 reads: "You did not treat me with contempt or scorn. Instead, you welcomed me as if I were an angel of God."

[6]While Galen was later (AD 130-210) the most famous of the Roman physicians, the earlier medical precedents were set by Hippocrates of Kos, an island off of the province of Asia, who lived from about 460-370 BC and set the standard of noninvasive care for centuries to come. From him we got the Hippocratic oath, about doing no harm.

he frequently quoted Jesus as saying 'a workman is worthy of his hire,' but he didn't want to become someone's client, which led to entangling alliances."

Prisca chuckled. "Paulus was nobody's hired after-dinner speaker addressing men at the *symposion*—or, in Latin, the *symposium*—who had had too much wine."[7]

"What were your meetings like, then?"

"I said that tongue in cheek. We did follow the pattern of a Greco-Roman meal when Erastus hosted our worship and *koinōnia* times in his large villa. There, Paulus would offer an oracle, or teaching from Torah. It was a fellowship of equals, and Erastus understood that Paulus was not his client."

Prisca paused as if remembering something. "Paulus first took the initiative to share the story of Christus with Erastus, who came around regularly to collect the rent.[8] It changed Erastus's life, but it also changed our social situation. Suddenly, we had a place to meet other than in our cramped quarters in the *subura*, just above the Odeon. Erastus's villa was on a side of the hill known as the Acrocorinth, and we would get there easily for weekly meetings and sometimes more." Prisca put a hand to her stomach. "But all this talk has made me hungry. Let's take a break and go to the market."

The trip to the market from Prisca's house was not a long one. When she was young, she and Priscilla would always go to the *Porticus Argonautarum* on the other side of central Roma, but that was too far a walk for Prisca's old knees, so instead she and Julia and Achilles shopped closer to home.

The problem was deciding which of the myriads of merchants to go and make purchases from. Even just in Prisca' district of Roma, dozens and dozens of shops greeted their eyes. Small shops and workshops like that of the tentmakers lined street after street, interspersed with *taberna*, some more raucous than others, and marble food counters at the fronts of some houses

---

[7] Julia knows her Latin, but very little Greek, so Priscilla must sometimes translate.
[8] Romans 16:23. See Ben Witherington III, *A Week in the Life of Corinth* (Downers Grove, IL: IVP Academic, 2012).

invited a person to lean there while someone dished up a bowl of soup and some warm bread with fish pickle sauce, or a bowl of nuts and dates.

Figure 7.1. Herculaneum was destroyed when Vesuvius erupted in AD 79.

The poet Martial was right that central Roma looked like one big shop, that is, until Domitianus decided—only shortly before Prisca began to tell her story—that many of the shops had to go, and so there followed a massive deconstruction and cleanup of the more flimsy and cheap establishments. Not surprisingly, the shops clustered around temples, public baths, and entertainment venues such as odeons, ampitheaters, circuses, and Titus's Colosseum. Prisca stopped at the garland maker's shop near the temple of Mars, as she wanted some flowers for the house. At the bakers' she got enough bread for the rest of the week and some pastries—two of which, stuffed with meat, Julia and Prisca made short work of while in the shop buying other things.

The olive merchant also received their business, as Prisca wanted several different types of olives, particularly some of the large black ones from the province of Achaea. She had developed a taste for them while living in Corinth. Chickpeas were also on the grocery list, in order to make a different spread for the bread, and also, some of the delicious cooked sausages with spices in them. Then they sought out the turbot, currently in good supply and fresh out of the water, not to mention a couple of amphorae of Falernian wine, the very best Italia had to offer. Achilles was pushing the small wheelbarrow that served as their shopping cart. Onto it he loaded the two amphorae and a few small packages, and the rest Prisca and Julia carried in large cloth bags: one for meats, one for breads, one for fruits. So preoccupied

were they with their shopping that none of them noticed the Roman soldier who seemed to be following them at a distance.

After the successful shopping trip, Julia and Prisca returned to the garden and to the task at hand. "That little excursion rekindled my sweeter memories," Prisca said to Julia. "I was so happy when Priscilla would take me with her to market, just the two of us." She put a hand on her daughter's. "Being with you there gives me the same feeling of belonging with someone all over again."

Figure 7.2. A bakery stall in the market.

Julia's eyes rimmed with tears, and she squeezed Prisca's hand. Something about telling this story was allowing her mother to open up to her in ways she'd seemed to find difficult before now.

"Ah, where were we?" Prisca said. "I remember that our lives changed dramatically when Paulus arrived with all his spiritual gifts and remarkable teaching. Most followers of Christus today think of Paulus as a great apostle, a person whose letters are weighty and powerful, a person who spread the good news right across the empire, and there is much truth in that. But Paulus was also a prophet and an ecstatic."

"And that was important in Corinth?"

Prisca nodded, so Julia asked, "Why?"

"Most Corinthians traveled up the mountain to the oracle at Delphi. But instead of having to go to the oracle, the oracle Paulus had come to them. When persons received Christus in Corinth they also received the Spirit

and numerous spiritual gifts that neither Aquila nor I had, gifts of prophesying and speaking in angelic tongues."

Julia was familiar with such gifts but wondered what it would be like to have experienced them when it first began happening. "That must have been astounding!"

Prisca nodded once slowly. "Yes

Figure 7.3. The Oracle of Delphi preparing to utter a prophecy.

. . . but the problem came because the Corinthians, who were over-

whelmingly Gentile, used those gifts the way the Pythia operated at Delphi, so worship turned into chaos. Lots of people spoke at once, some prophesying, some speaking in tongues, and eventually Paulus had to write a stern letter to correct all the abuses, not to mention all sorts of other problems of immorality. He tried to enforce, with only some success, Jacob's decree about staying away from the pagan temples where idolatry and immorality were rife."[9]

---

[9]Prisca is referring to the decree in Acts 15, which is not about imposing a modicum of Jewish food laws on Gentiles; it's about their staying away from pagan temple feasts where the four things listed would be found together. The problem is mainly an issue of venue not menu, and Paulus understood this well, as he tells the Corinthians they can eat whatever meat they find in the market in Corinth without issues of conscience, even though much of it came from the pagan

Prisca fell silent for so long, cast back in memory to that very time and place, that Julia reluctantly interjected: "Back to how things began in Corinth?"

Prisca smiled. "Of course. I seem to be having trouble keeping on task as I recall Corinth. It was such an adjustment in my life."

She stood up and stretched to clear her mind, then sat back down to continue. "Paulus was already a seasoned evangelist when he came to us. He'd taken the good news to many provinces and cities, such as Galatia, Troas, Philippi, and Thessaloniki. There were small successes at Berea and a few converts at Athens, too, before Paulus came knocking on our door.

"With this behind him, Paulus had a regular procedure worked out. He would start in the synagogues, appealing to the entire congregation to accept Jesus as the Jewish messiah. It was Paulus's conviction that the gospel was for the Jew first."[10]

Julia was curious: "Was that a good method?"

Prisca thought a moment before she answered. "Jews were not looking for a crucified messiah that rose from the dead, and Gentiles often thought this was some sort of eastern religion's foolishness or nonsense. The message itself was problematic—never mind the character of the messenger. And yet, and yet . . . God used it to bring a goodly number of people to the Lord. It was nothing short of a miracle, and a miraculous outpouring of the Spirit and spiritual gifts accompanied it. Honestly, I'd not seen anything like it since Pentecost some thirty-seven years prior."

Julia looked at her mentor, admiration mixed with envy at the marvels she'd been witness to. Her contemplation couldn't last long, for Prisca continued.

"We hadn't planned to get caught up in a vast effort to evangelize the Roman Empire; to the contrary, we'd planned to practice our trade and lay low until Claudius ceased being emperor in Roma, so we could go home. But it was clear that Paulus needed help."

---

temple sacrifices, but they must stay away from the dinner parties in the temples, where the gods were thought to dwell, and even to participate in the feasts (1 Corinthians 8-10).
[10]Romans 1:16.

"He didn't have any help besides you?"

"Yes, there was Timothy, and then later Titus, but one thing Paulus especially needed was a woman who could go places where only women went, and talk to women in ways that would appeal specifically to them. In short, he especially needed someone like me who was fluent in both Greek and Latin."

"Domina, I've heard some say that Paulus silenced women and prevented them from using their God-given gifts."

Prisca shook her head vehemently. "This is far from the truth. In Corinth, he corrected women who were interrupting the worship service with questions for those prophesying, but that mistake was understandable since the Greek tradition is to ask an oracle pertinent personal questions to get guidance for the future. But in his second letter to the Corinthians, written from Ephesus, Paulus endorsed women praying and prophesying in the worship, as any reader of it should clearly understand."[11]

Clearly this was a sore subject with Prisca. She took a few calming breaths. "There was also a problem in Ephesus with high-status women, recently converted from Greek religion, particularly the worship of Artemis, wanting to immediately be able to teach in our assembly there. But Paulus had to explain that they must first listen and learn the good news well before they could teach.[12] Because of assumptions about their own status, several of them attempted to take over one of our house meetings, which caused chaos.[13] But Paulus was correcting problems, not forbidding women from teaching or proclaiming the good news. Indeed, he was a big promoter of my doing so."

Julia was pondering these interesting facts when Prisca abruptly changed subjects. "It was a combination of factors that led to Paulus being summoned

---

[11] 1 Corinthians. Note that Paul mentions in 1 Corinthians 5 a letter he wrote before he wrote the one we call 1 Corinthians.

[12] See for instance Gary Hoag, *Wealth in Ancient Ephesus and the First Letter to Timothy* (University Park, PA: Eisenbrauns, 2015).

[13] 1 Timothy 2:8-15.

before the proconsul Gallio in central Corinth to face charges—after he had been in Corinth well over a year."

"What? Who's Gallio?" Julia said, thinking a moment. "Didn't he live in Roma some years ago?"

Prisca nodded as she saw light dawn in Julia's expression. "Indeed, you should remember him. Junius Annaeus Gallio was his full Roman name, but his origins were in Spain. He was the son of Seneca the Elder, brother to Nero's advisor, also called Seneca. While Gallio could be charming in social interaction, he had few skills in administration and even less patience in dealing with the tedium of governing. And then there was the fact that he was literally plagued by something in the air in Corinth and hated being there. His doctors said he was ruled by his bile or gall. As a result, he wasn't well nor in good humor while there. He didn't suffer fools gladly, and like many Romans, he didn't like Jews.

"Julia, I'm sure I don't need to tell you that Roman law is heavily biased in favor of Roman citizens, and so the straw that broke the camel's back was over Paulus' converting Crispus, one of the leaders of the synagogue of the Hebrews. It was one thing to convert a lesser member of the synagogue. It was quite another when Crispus and his family converted.

"And so when Gallio discerned this was a squabble over Jewish religious ideas, and when he learned that Paulus was a Roman citizen, and that Sosthenes, the synagogue leader who brought the charges against Paulus, was *not* a Roman citizen, Gallio threw the case out of court and told them to settle the matter privately. Sosthenes ended up being beaten by his own people for shaming them before the Roman authorities. The irony is, he too ended up converting to the new faith and volunteered to be Paulus's scribe, even traveling with us to Ephesus and penning Paulus's second letter back to Corinth. It was a tumultuous time, to say the least. But it was exciting in good ways too."

Prisca fell silent again. Julia almost hated to interrupt her reverie, but she was getting bolder about keeping the story moving. "What were some problems in the church?"

It worked. Prisca continued: "We met in several different homes, which caused divisions among us. And there were no elders, deacons, or overseers. When one couples this with the enthusiastic nature of Corinthian worship, full of speaking in tongues, prophesying, long meals where some even got drunk during the Lord's Supper—well, you can see we needed some better local leadership to produce order out of the chaos."

"So where is the line, Domina, between keeping order and quenching the Spirit?

"That's a difficult subject, and if I get on that we'll never finish this tale!"

Julia smiled and had to agree. "Okay, back to the story. What happened after Paulus's trial?"

"Paulus had much experience and could see there would be more trouble, not least because a second synagogue ruler, Stephanus, and his whole household had been converted. Paulus baptized them down by the sea in the eastern port of Cencherae, a bit away from the prying eyes in central Corinth. That's when Paulus met a high-status woman named Phoebe, who came to watch the baptism since it was near her coastal home in Cencherae. When Paulus returned to Corinth some years later, she was a house assembly leader, like Lydia in Philippi, and he stayed in her home. In fact, Paulus named her the first proper *diakonos* of the assembly of God in Corinth, and even later she was to have the honor of taking Paulus's famous Roman letter to Roma and reading it aloud there. But I get ahead of myself."

"So how did you end up going with Paulus to Ephesus?"

"After a year of Paulus being with us in Corinth, making tents and converts, he felt compelled to go to Ephesus and asked us to be his coworkers. We prayed, fasted, and waited on guidance from the Lord, and agreed to go with him. Both of us were apprehensive, as we'd never done anything like

that before. We liked working behind the scenes for Christus, not being the public face of our movement. So this was far from comfortable and natural. We left our shop in Erastus's hands. He put his able freedman Nicanor in charge while we were gone."[14]

"Were you scared?" Julia asked.

"Yes, but you know how you get a feeling of certainty when you know something is right? Aquila and I had that feeling when we agreed to go with Paulus, even though it was an unknown and potentially hostile situation.

"However, after asking us to come with him, Paulus felt he must first sail back to Syria and down to Jerusalem to report on things in the eastern empire. In preparation for his visit to Jerusalem, which he faced with some trepidation, he took a Nazaritic vow and had Phoebe cut his hair before boarding the ship."[15]

"Domina, explain to me a Naziritic vow. I've heard the term, but I don't understand it."

"A Naziritic vow is something described in the Torah.[16] The word *nazir* means consecrated, and it's when a person devotes himself to the Lord, abstaining entirely from the fruit of the vine; so, wine, grapes, and raisins. He also allows his hair to grow long and vows not to touch a corpse or a tomb for the period of the vow. John the Baptizer seems to have maintained a Naziritic vow throughout his ministry, but most take one for a specific period of time, as Paulus did. Paulus did not think long hair was appropriate on a man and so cut his just before starting the vow."[17]

Just as Prisca finished this portion of the story, someone knocked on her door. Clemens opened it to find a Roman soldier standing there, tall and strong, in full regalia. "Does a woman named Priscilla or Prisca live here?" he asked in a commanding tone.

---

[14]A part of his story is told in Witherington, *A Week in the Life of Corinth*.
[15]Acts 18:18.
[16]Numbers 6:1-21.
[17]On Paul's views on men with long hair see 1 Corinthians 11:14—he saw it as contrary to nature, whereas he saw long hair on women as their "glory."

With some trepidation, Clemens nodded and said, "Yes, what do you want?"

"She is to appear before a tribunal set up by the god and ruler Domitianus. We are investigating religious crimes and crimes of sedition," the soldier said.

Clemens swallowed hard and said, "Surely you don't need an old woman for such a tribunal."

"We have reports she aided Paulus whom Nero executed. We need to investigate to see if she has continued criminal practices, like cannibalism and defaming the emperor. I'll be here tomorrow to collect her. Have her ready, and do not even think about hiding her or warning her to flee. We've been watching for some time, and she seems in perfectly good health. Good enough to walk to market and back anyway. Until tomorrow—Hail Domitianus," the soldier said.

Julia and Prisca overheard all of this, and Julia looked to Prisca, alarmed. "What are you going to do?" she asked.

But Prisca only patted her shoulder and said, "It will be alright. I have some help in high places."

By this time Clemens was also looking intently at Prisca, so she instructed him: "Ask Achilles to go to Caesar's household. There are many Christus followers right under Domitianus's nose, both slaves and freedmen.[18] Tell them what's happened. Since they're in charge of the documents for such tribunals, ask them to see if they can delay my appearance at the tribunal, at least until I can finish our story of the earliest Christus followers in Roma."

Clemens looked relieved and said, "At once, Domina. I'll ask Achilles to go immediately and speak to Herodion. He's elderly but still in favor with the emperor. We'll sort this out."

---

[18]Romans 16 indicates there were Christ followers already a part of Caesar's household in Nero's day, as does Philippians 4. Both the Praetorian guard (Philippians 1) and Caesar's household had Christ followers among them already in the AD 60s.

8

ON TO EPHESUS

The council and people honored Claudia Polla Quintilla, the kaueis,
for having served with dignity as priestess of the goddess [Artemis] for
having provided all things needful with due devotion and munificence,
for having displayed reverence towards the goddess and public spirit
toward the community; and for having zealously performed at her
own cost the public sacrifices performed each month by the city; in
the year when Stertinius Quartus was proconsul.

The council and the people honored and erected a statue to Apphion,
Demetrius' daughter, the kaueis the priestess of Artemis.

INSCRIPTIONS FOUND IN SARDIS

ACHILLES WAS ABLE TO CONVINCE Herodion to delay the inevitable
by a good month. To everyone's relief, Publius, the centurion, did not return
the next day. The official reason for the delay was cited as "incomplete

---

Inscriptions Found in Sardis: W.H. Buckler and D.M. Robinson, "Greek Inscriptions from Sardes
III," *American Journal of Archaeology* 17 (1913): 353-57.

documents." Caesar's household excelled at many things, none more so than piling up the papyri and slowing down official processes![1]

Prisca now felt the urgency of completing her story, with potentially little time and forty plus years to chronicle. Her words came to Julia in a rush, and the younger woman did her best to keep pace with her stylus.

Figure 8.1. The once great Temple of Artemis in Ephesus. All that is left is one column standing in a swamp.

"The journey by boat from Corinth to Ephesus was some 250 Roman sea miles. It was much faster than traveling 1500 miles by Roman road through Greece to Macedonia, then sailing to Troas, and walking down to Ephesus from there.

"We took a trunk of our belongings once more, though we also left some things behind with Titius, not knowing exactly how long we might be in Ephesus. After all, Paulus had been expelled rather quickly from some of the cities where he preached. But Paulus was not interested in leaving a bunch of half-converted persons in his wake. And so it was that we spent almost three years in Ephesus. Paulus actually left us there with specific instructions to lay the groundwork for his mission in that city while he went on to Jerusalem."

---

[1]On Caesar's household and the Christ followers in it, see Philippians 4:22.

Prisca stopped and popped an olive in her mouth, chewing and thinking, so Julia took the opportunity to ask, "How was Ephesus different from Corinth?"

Prisca swallowed and thought for a moment. "The character and climate of Ephesus was *quite* different from Corinth. For one thing, it was still a Greek city, not a Roman colony, and it had a huge temple of Artemis that attracted pilgrims and ordinary tourists who came to gawk at the buildings, whether they were interested in the religion or not. I liked Ephesus far better than Corinth in various regards, not least because women there had a good deal of freedom, including religious freedom that the empire had not taken away. Ephesus, or *Ephesos* as the Greeks called it, was the most famous city in the province of Asia, and its name means bee, hence the coins with pictures of bees and also a stag, the animal associated with Artemis, or Diana, the goddess of the hunt and of fertility.

Figure 8.2. Coins that represent Ephesus and Artemis.

"Artemis was not just the goddess of human fertility but also the goddess of crop and animal fertility. Many of the pilgrims to the festivals in honor of Artemis came to ask for or thank her for a good crop,

Figure 8.3. Artemis was the goddess of the hunt and fertility.

children, or a good hunt. The temple of Artemis was a huge part of the economy there, even for the silversmiths who made little replicas of the temple. Any criticism of the temple was seen as bad for business."

"So did that make things difficult for Paulus?"

"Eventually. But the good thing was that they were open to religion and new ideas, which allowed Paulus to rent a hall off Curetes Street in the older part of Ephesus, not far from the markets. The hall belonged to a man named Tyrannus, who did not much care who paid him to use it, so long as the money came in. Rhetoricians and philosophers regularly spoke there and drew a crowd, so Paulus could use the hall only in early afternoon, right when people wanted a little rest after midday meals.

"Oh, Julia, I failed to mention the beastly moisture in the air during an Ephesus summer. It was miserably humid. Plus, two large hills blocked breezes from the harbor all the way up Curetes Street. So, the hours just after the midday were steamy. But Paulus only rented this hall on his return to Ephesus, after being in Jerusalem for some months."

Figure 8.4. The Celsus library was built in the second century AD.

"Back to whether ministry was hard in Ephesus. If I were to use one word to describe the religious character of Ephesus, it would be *cross-fertilization*. Here were Hellenized Jews, partially Judaized Greeks, Romans who honored both the traditional gods and the emperor, and many practitioners of the dark arts—various forms of magic, necromancy, witchcraft, divining, the reading of animal's entrails. Many sold spells, magic books, curse formulas, and blessing prayers. It's not surprising that many Romans who came to Ephesus called it 'the center of *superstitio.*' There were all sorts of fantastic religious ideas and practices. This is one reason followers of Christus did not necessarily stand out from the crowd. 'Just another strange eastern religion,' people would say. None of this seemed to faze Paulus when he shared the good news. He saw competition and even opposition as a positive challenge, but he had faith the Word would change people if it was clearly and persuasively presented."

"Yes!" Julia interjected with enthusiasm. "I remember in one of his letters, he spoke of the kind welcome he got. I was impressed when he mentioned how they turned to God from idols to serve a living and true God and to wait for his Son from heaven. His exact words were 'And we also thank God continually because, when you received the word of God, which you heard from us, you accepted it not as a human word, but as it actually is, the word of God, which is indeed at work in you who believe.'"[2]

"Indeed! Well done, Julia. Paulus had no doubt he was truly proclaiming God's good news, and that its message would change many into Christus followers. And he would not let anything, not persecution, not incarceration, not beatings, not shipwrecks, not opposition from Jews, or Gentiles, or Roman officials, deter him. I've never met a person so utterly confident and convinced that he was doing God's will and saying God's prophetic word. He was surely a servant of God, but he also was like a force of nature—rather

---

[2] 1 Thessalonians.1:9-10; 2:13.

unstoppable and certainly irrepressible. We don't need to put this in our chronicle, but I read his words to the Corinthians just this morning. Do you mind if I read them?"

Julia put her stylus down and shook her hand to loosen the muscles. "Please do. I need a break."

Prisca unrolled a scroll, which was set beside her, and read in a clear, sure voice: "But we have this treasure in jars of clay to show that this all-surpassing power is from God and not from us. We are hard pressed on every side, but not crushed; perplexed, but not in despair; persecuted, but not abandoned; struck down, but not destroyed. We always carry around in our body the death of Jesus, so that the life of Jesus may also be revealed in our body. For we who are alive are always being given over to death for Jesus' sake, so that his life may also be revealed in our mortal body. So then, death is at work in us, but life is at work in you. . . . Therefore, we do not lose heart. Though outwardly we are wasting away, yet inwardly we are being renewed day by day. For our light and momentary troubles are achieving for us an eternal glory that far outweighs them all. So, we fix our eyes not on what is seen, but on what is unseen, since what is seen is temporary, but what is unseen is eternal."[3]

"I see what you mean," said Julia. "I've never met such a man, but then I haven't lived as long as you." She was quiet for a few moments, her eyes on her tablet, pondering. "While I never knew Paulus, what I do know is I'm thankful that you, his coworker, took me into your home, your life, your family, and gave me an education, a trade, and a home. I don't remember how it began, but I'm so grateful."

Prisca took the tablet from Julia and set it beside the scroll. She took both of her daughter's hands in her own and waited until the younger woman's eyes met hers. "Julia. *My* Julia. You are as dear to me as if you

---

[3] 2 Corinthians 4:7-12, 16-18.

were my own offspring, so the joy is all mine." She paused and, thinking of the summons to the emperor, added, "If anything should happen to me, I have made sure everything I own will pass to you. I want your life to be good—and as rich as Priscilla and Aquila and Paulus, and *you*, have made my own life to be."

An awkward pause settled between them as Julia remained silent, almost afraid to move. But then it was replaced by a stillness, a peace that she couldn't quite name, even as she understood she'd been hoping to hear these words her entire life. She *had* sensed Prisca's love for her many, many times, but the good woman had never put her feelings so forthrightly. The sensation was more than she'd ever known, both filling her heart and passing through and far beyond her, connecting her to a wholeness that she might have named the Spirit making its home with her.

9

ENTER APOLLOS

*Meanwhile a Jew named Apollos, a native of Alexandria, came to
Ephesus. He was a learned man, with a thorough knowledge of the
Scriptures. He had been instructed in the way of the Lord, and he
spoke with great fervor and taught about Jesus accurately, though
he knew only the baptism of John. He began to speak boldly in the
synagogue. When Priscilla and Aquila heard him, they invited him
to their home and explained to him the way of God more adequately.*

ACTS 18:24-26

*Apollo was that rare deity who had the same name for the Greeks
and the Romans. He was the god of the sun, but also of music and
prophecy, and was the patron of the oracle at Delphi, who claimed
to be inspired by him. Persons named for this deity were expected to
do remarkable things including having remarkable gifts of speaking,
for instance, about matters religious.*

PRISCA HELD ONTO JULIA'S HANDS until she could see that her
words had struck deeper than she'd known they would. She removed her
hands and watched them smooth her own *stola,* to give her daughter some

sense of privacy in this moment. The open look on Julia's face made Prisca ashamed—ashamed that she'd said anything to cause Julia to be so openly affected by the words, and more so that she hadn't said anything like this to her daughter until now. To spare her daughter any further discomfort—or perhaps herself, if she were being completely honest—all Prisca knew to do was continue the story she had already begun.

"So, we had been in Ephesus some time, indeed long enough to establish one assembly of Christus followers in our own home. Paulus, according to a report from Timothy, had finished his time in Jerusalem, gone up to Antioch in Syria, and then decided he must check on his churches in Galatia before coming to Ephesus. So we were still waiting for the arrival of the great 'apostle to the Gentiles.' But we were not idle, and things became much more interesting when a formidable man named Apollos disembarked from a boat from Alexandria."

"What made Apollos so unique?"

"Probably not one tenth of all humanity in the empire had his education, learning, and sheer eloquence. Not only did he know the Scriptures, but he was an expert in the art of persuasion. He could project wonderfully and drew a crowd after speaking just a few sentences of elegant and eloquent Greek. Not surprisingly, the Greeks in Ephesus, who loved a good rhetorician, became enraptured with Apollos almost immediately. He could have discoursed on the number of angels that could stand on my loom's shuttlecock, and they would have listened."

Julia chuckled at this mental picture, Prisca grinning back.

"We first ran into him at the synagogue, where he pointed out that the suffering servant in Isaiah was in fact Jesus of Nazareth! It was brilliant, and convinced some, but we noticed he left something out.

"Once the service was over, we approached Apollo and introduced ourselves. We asked whether he knew 'the way of the Lord,' which means responding to the call of the good news by being baptized in Jesus' name. To our surprise, he freely admitted he had only heard of John's baptism. So, over a nice meal at our favorite little food stand on the south side of Ephesus, we instructed him more accurately in 'the way of the Lord.' As you'll remember, the early name for our movement was 'the Way' and so it was quite natural for us to call the initiation rite, or the way into the community, 'the way of the Lord' since a person was baptized in Jesus' name."

Julia interrupted. "Why just the name of Jesus, and not also the name of the Father and the Spirit?"

Prisca was clearly pleased at this question, satisfied that Julia had learned to think carefully. "The answer is simple—all the earliest converts, including Apollos, already believed in the God of the Bible. It was Jesus into which they needed to be inducted and baptized. Jesus was the new thing in their faith and practice. Paulus would later explain that the Spirit baptized people into the body of Christus, the living organism of God's people joined to each other and to their head, Christus himself. Water baptism symbolized the death of the old person, which led to the baptism by the Spirit into the new body, the new person—Christus himself."[1]

"That makes sense. So did you get to know Apollos well?"

"Yes. We soon became fast friends, and he stayed some weeks with us in Ephesus. When he finally moved on, he asked the assembly in our house to provide a letter of reference to the household congregations in Corinth so that he could go, as he put it, 'Do some watering where Paulus and you two have planted the word.' We were glad to do so, but it was a bit of a shame that he missed Paulus's arrival in Ephesus by only a week."

"Only a week!"

"Only a week. But our encounter with Apollos reminded us that God's Spirit was directing our movement, not some human leader like Jacob or Peter, or even the Jerusalem mother assembly. Apollos had heard the good

---

[1]On this, see Romans 6:1-5, and also 1 Corinthians 12.

news through another one of those Jews who had been at Pentecost in Jerusalem. Ours was not a movement based primarily on human calculations and plans, though some of that was important and necessary. It was God's Spirit who led, guided, guarded, and even goaded us into sharing the faith wherever we went. This is a fact we should never forget.

"One more thing about Apollos. Many of the rhetoric-hungry Corinthians liked Apollos's eloquence better than Paulus's skills. This wasn't because Paulus was not a good rhetorician; his letters show he was. But Apollos had no ethos problems; indeed, he was a handsome younger man who actually looked like his namesake, with golden-bronze skin and the tongue of an oracle and a rhetor. The Corinthians, even at their best, tended to be partisans, and some began to say 'I am of Paulus,' others 'I am of Apollos,' and Paulus had to quell this too singular focus on a particular human leader. Apollos's arrival in Corinth unintentionally set the rivalry conventions in motion. To his credit, Apollos never encouraged this. In fact, he was a bit naïve about the human tendency to latch onto the eloquent and charismatic ones. So, when Apollos had come and gone from Corinth and later learned he had something of a 'personal following' there, as they clamored for his return, he declined for a good period of time, so as not to further exacerbate some sort of rivalry against Paulus's or our work in Corinth. Instead, he returned to Ephesus and our fellowship where he finally met Paulus, the apostle he had heard so much about."[2]

"He sounds like a remarkable man."

"He was. But most of all he served a remarkable God."

---

[2] 1 Corinthians 16:12.

10

DEMONS AND DARK ARTS IN EPHESUS

When he came to power in AD 69, Vespasian outlawed astrology. However, because of his personal friendship with the famous Ephesian astrologer, Balbillus, Ephesus was allowed to continue to hold sacred games in his honor. Artemis' temple in Ephesus was considered one of the seven wonders of the world and it was also a sponsor of the magic arts.

BEFORE THEY BEGAN THE NEXT DAY, Prisca held up a small piece of parchment. "Julia, I found this little curse roll in the temple of Asclepius in Corinth. Aquila and I had been commissioned to make some tents for the upcoming Isthmian games season, as the temple was expecting some special guests from Athens. We were delivering two of these smaller tents, made of goat's hair cloth or *cilicium*,[1] and I found this on the floor of the antechamber to the priest's quarters, where we were to meet the purchaser. I shuddered when I opened it and read the inscription."

She unrolled it and said, "After several formulaic names of deities, it says,

---

[1] *Cilicium* became the word for the cloth that tents were made of, because it came from Paulus's native region, Cilicia, and Cilicia was famous for its goat's hair cloth.

'May Aurora be cursed. May her womb be closed and never again opened. May she suffer much bleeding during her time of bleeding. May she become sickly and never recover, for stealing my man.' The belief behind these little curse rolls is that if they can get close to the deity, they are more likely to be effective."

"What a terrible sentiment of hate! Thank goodness we are not under the sway of that religion!"

Prisca agreed. "As Aquila used to say, 'Human beings are inherently religious, and the only alternative to good religion is not no religion, but rather bad religion.'"

"What a perceptive thing to say! I wish I'd had more time to know him."

"I know, dear. Me too."

They both sat quietly, missing the man that Prisca knew intimately and that Julia barely remembered. Finally, Prisca sighed and continued. "We faced every permutation and combination of superstition imaginable in Ephesus."

"Can you give me an example?"

"For instance, astrology. While even Jews and followers of Jesus believe the stars affect human life in various ways, Aquila used to say '*astra inclinant, sed non obligant*'—'While the stars may incline us in some direction, they do not obligate us.' Inclination is not the same as determination. Some have speculated whether stars are actually beings, the heavenly host, so to speak. The Bible does say that God's messengers, the heavenly hosts, can influence us."

Julia had never heard this idea. "Do you think that's true?"

"I have no idea. We know nothing about the stars. Anyway, what I had not expected was some of the more bizarre combinations of Jewish faith with magic or the dark arts."

"That can be difficult," Julia admitted. "Where *is* the dividing line between magic and miracle?"

Prisca pondered that a moment. "Magic or the dark arts, as I understand them, are human attempts to control some deity and gain special power or help thereby, part of the human endeavor to control life and its circumstances. Miracle on the other hand is something God does and cannot be manipulated or controlled by humans."

Julia seemed satisfied with that answer.

"There was an occasion when several odd things happened when Paulus interacted with local Jews and magicians in Ephesus. Julia, would you get the second scroll written by Luke? I want a small section of it in our chronicle."

Julia was gone for some minutes, and came back with a large container of scrolls. "I wasn't sure which scroll you wanted. Was it the second chronicle written to Theophilus?"

"Yes that's the one. Hand it to me, please."

Prisca unrolled it until she came to the last third of the scroll, reading out loud as she went to find the place she wanted. Like most documents it was written in *scriptio continua*, a continuous flow of Greek letters without separation of words, phrases, sentences, or paragraphs.

With some satisfaction, she finally said "Aha! Here it is. I'll read it: 'God did extraordinary miracles through Paulus, so that even handkerchiefs and aprons that had touched him were taken to the sick, and their illnesses were cured and the evil spirits left them. Some Jews who went around driving out evil spirits tried to invoke the name of the Lord Jesus over those who were demon-possessed. They would say, "In the name of the Jesus whom Paulus preaches, I command you to come out." Seven sons of Sceva, a Jewish chief priest, were doing this. One day the evil spirit answered them, "Jesus I know, and Paulus I know about, but who are you?" Then the man who had the evil spirit jumped on them and overpowered them all. He gave them such a beating that they ran out of the house naked and bleeding.'"[2]

---

[2] Acts 19:11-16.

"Now what do you make of this, Julia?"

Julia hesitated and said, "I'm not sure, but it sounds frightening. I've never witnessed an exorcism."

"Nor do you want to, if you want to sleep at night. The story is meant to exalt Paulus the holy man, so holy that even things he touched could convey healing and exorcism. In contrast, the Jewish exorcists had to borrow Jesus' name."

Prisca grinned. "Luke had a good sense of humor as well; I still laugh at that line 'Jesus I know, and Paulus I know—but who in the world are you?' Luke tries to show that such attempts at controlling Jesus' power were ridiculous. Without a close, positive relationship with Jesus, it's better not to invoke his name to accomplish a sign miracle. I believe in the existence of evil spirits, but I don't believe a person who hasn't the gift of exorcism should try and dabble in such things. This story shows what a bad idea this is. The whole thing can go terribly wrong. The exorcist could end up needing exorcism!"[3]

Julia shuddered. "Ugh! Let's move on in this story."

"Surely. I forgot to read the positive outcome of that bizarre encounter, which I was thankful not to witness personally. Here is Luke's conclusion: 'When this became known to the Jews and Greeks living in Ephesus, they were all seized with fear, and the name of the Lord Jesus was held in high honor. Many of those who believed now came and openly confessed what they had done. A number who had practiced sorcery brought their scrolls together and burned them publicly. When they calculated the value of the scrolls, the total came to fifty thousand drachmas. In this way, the word of the Lord spread widely and grew in power.'"[4]

---

[3]What then of the strange exorcist in Mark 9:38-40 who was not a disciple? Presumably, he was not merely trying to manipulate the power of Jesus but had a positive assessment of Jesus' miracle working and was imitating him or the disciples. Jesus suggests he is "for us" and thus not a mere manipulator.

[4]Acts 19:17-20.

"That's incredible!"

"Yes, but Julia, there's a difference between a holy fear or reverence of the living God and a fear of the holy, of the supernatural in general. The story does not say those hearing of this remarkable incident became followers of Jesus. They just believed the name of Jesus had some kind of incredible power, and it frightened them. But that terror actually led some to come and confess, and even some of the sorcerers came to repentance and voluntarily burned their own incantation scrolls and magical formulae. Not only does true religion expose false religion, it can lead people to forsake false religion."

"Thanks be to God!"

"Indeed. God is not at our beck and call as if we are the masters and he the powerful servant. No—quite the opposite. We are God's servants, but he graciously chooses to hear our prayers and use us for good and godly purposes."

"That seems like a good place to stop, Domina. I need to think about this truth for a while."

"Yes, enough for this day; we need to say our prayers and get some rest."

Prisca slept soundly, even though she still worried about the summons to a tribunal. She'd just heard that Flavia Domitilla had been exiled from Roma in recent days for being a follower of Christus, and this frightened Prisca, because Flavia was a high-status woman, and was even related to Domitianus.[5] But she realized that sometimes sleep was the best medicine for her cares, and she had long practice in casting her cares on the Lord before shutting her eyes.

---

[5]See the discussion in Peter Lampe, *From Paul to Valentinus: Christians at Rome in the First Two Centuries* (Minneapolis, MN: Fortress, 2003), 198-205. Her exile, which began in AD 96, lasted less than a year, and Nerva apparently restored her fortunes when she returned.

11

RIOT IN THE THEATER, WILD BEASTS IN EPHESUS

If I fought wild beasts in Ephesus with no more than human hopes,
what have I gained? If the dead are not raised,

> *"Let us eat and drink,*
> *for tomorrow we die."*

Do not be misled: "Bad company corrupts good character."

PAULUS

What are you? A human being. If you see yourself as something else,
it is natural for you to want to live to an old age, to be rich, and to
enjoy health. But if you regard yourself as human and as a part of the
whole, for the sake of the whole you may have to suffer an illness, make
a voyage and run risks, be in want, and even die before your time.

EPICTETUS, *DISCOURSES* 2.5.25-26

Quotation from Paulus: 1 Corinthians 15:32-33. Paul is here quoting Isaiah 22:13 and the Greek poet Menander.

Julia felt that each day started earlier and with a greater sense of urgency. She yawned, trying to fully wake herself as Prisca started her narrative once more.

"It was neither Paulus's exorcisms in Ephesus nor even his prompting of burning magic books that really turned many there against him. Rather it was his interfering with the business of selling trinkets and the suggestion that Artemis was no deity—indeed that Artemis never existed as a deity! This got him into all sorts of hot water; so much so that he had to leave town in a hurry.

"This is when I finally had an argument with Paulus. I told him he had to go, pushed him out the door of the tenement Aquila and I shared with him, and said that today was not a good day to become a martyr; there was too much ministry work still to be done. He argued with me all the way down the steps from the second floor, while Aquila was tying up his pack.

Figure 11.1. The famous theater in Ephesus.

When we reached street level you could still hear them chanting in the stadium 'Great is Artemis, Great is Artemis' with the sound wafting up the valley, and we were a good half mile away! I could see a crowd forming toward the bottom of Curetes Street, and someone said, 'There he is! Let's get him!'"

Suddenly Julia was wide awake.

"With the help of two friends as human shields we hastened up Curetes Street with four of us surrounding Paulus and hoping no one recognized him at the top of the hill. At the head of the valley we turned left and headed down the processional route that led to the Temple of Artemis.

"The Roman road was only about a mile out of town, and we hoped to reach it before chaos broke loose and some town authority came to arrest Paulus. Finally, he stopped arguing and put his head down. He set his face like a flint and wouldn't look us in the eyes but accepted our wisdom. We said farewell, and kept walking in the right direction.

"As we returned to the city, we ran into Homer, the town clerk, heading up Curetes Street. He knew us from our shop and wore a grim expression. 'You two are coming with me. Your man Paulus created a riot, and I had to calm things down in the arena. And you are not even citizens of Ephesus! I could put you on trial right now for sedition and rabble rousing.'

"I kept calm. 'You could, but we just hustled Paulus out of town. He won't be bothering you anymore. Besides, he's a Roman citizen and so am I, so let's not go through the arduous process of visiting with the proconsul and starting a trial, when you know I can appeal to Caesar and stop the trial instantly.'

"'So he's gone, gone for good?' Homer asked me.

"'Certainly gone for now,' I said, 'so let the crowds disperse and the noise cease, and things will go back to the way you want them, with peace and quiet for one and all.'

"This seemed to satisfy the worried man.

"And then Aquila said, 'By the way, I heard from an Asiarch[1] who was present that you gave quite the rhetorically effective speech in the theater. He said it was powerful.'

"Homer, brightened at this. 'Well I'm just glad it worked,' he said modestly, but he couldn't hold back a grin at the praise.

"Aquila returned his expression. 'Excellent deliberative rhetoric. So glad it worked so that our friends were not stoned or worse. Keeping the peace is important.'

"'So true,' Homer agreed. 'Thank you for hustling the troublemaker out of town before all Hades broke loose.'"

Julia loved this account. "You must have been so relieved!"

"You have no idea! I almost collapsed when it was over. That was a close one."

"So what did the followers of Christus do after Paulus's sudden exit? What happened to the public discourses in the hall of Tyrannus?"

"We kept quiet for a time, but then one of our number named Odysseus said there was a cave high above the slope houses of the rich near the hall of Tyrannus and that we could freely meet there. Only goatherds occasionally wandered into that terrain. And so the assembly of God in Ephesus held some of its meetings there in the evenings. That was where I first met a re-markable woman named Thecla. She had met Paulus in Iconium in the province of Galatia and had never married, but devoted herself to prayer, fasting, and proclaiming the good news.[2] She was also something of an oracle.

"One of the things that happened in the Pauline portion of our movement is that there were quite a few prophesying women, including Thecla. But like Paulus, Thecla was itinerant, yet she shared the story of Jesus primarily with other women. To this day, the movement has included such prophe-sying women, though I'm not one of them. My gifts are support and teaching."

---

[1] A title given to men of certain high honorary rank in the province of Asia, they were delegates of individual cities to the provincial council that regulated the worship of Rome and of the emperor.
[2] Her story is told in the second century document called *The Acts of Paul and Thecla*.

"Tell me more about the role of prophecy."

"To some extent, we don't need writing prophets as those in the Torah because we live in the age of prophecy fulfillment, so we searched the Scriptures for explanations of what was happening among us, rather than concentrating on trying to generate new prophecies. There were exceptions to this general truth, but not many. For one thing, Paulus urged us to sift and

Figure 11.2. A black and white photo of the painting in a cave above Ephesus that depicts Paul and Thecla.

weigh the prophecies, and for another he warned in his famous letter to the Romans that a prophet or prophetess should only prophesy according the measure or limits of his or her faith.[3] I took this double warning, to mean that prophecies after the time of Jesus were mainly specific utterances for specific persons—words of comfort, encouragement, hope—*and* they needed to be carefully weighed, as sometimes a prophet's enthusiasm might outstrip his inspiration. In any case, such prophecies mostly did not warrant or need to be written down or treated as sacred writings, unlike the many books of prophecies in Torah. Prophecy functioned differently once Christus had come and the fulfillments began."

---

[3]See 1 Corinthians 14 on the weighing of the prophecies, and Romans 12:6 on prophesying in proportion to one's faith.

12

RETURN TO GREECE

We do not want you to be uninformed, brothers and sisters, about the troubles we experienced in the province of Asia. We were under great pressure, far beyond our ability to endure, so that we despaired of life itself. Indeed, we felt we had received the sentence of death. But this happened that we might not rely on ourselves but on God, who raises the dead. He has delivered us from such a deadly peril, and he will deliver us again.

2 CORINTHIANS 1:8-10

Now when I went to Troas to preach the gospel of Christ and found that the Lord had opened a door for me, I still had no peace of mind, because I did not find my brother Titus there. So I said goodbye to them and went on to Macedonia.

But thanks be to God, who always leads us as captives in Christ's triumphal procession and uses us to spread the aroma of the knowledge of him everywhere. For we are to God the pleasing aroma of Christ among those who are being saved and those who are perishing. To the one we are an aroma that brings death; to the other, an aroma that

brings life. And who is equal to such a task? Unlike so many, we do
not peddle the word of God for profit. On the contrary, in Christ we
speak before God with sincerity, as those sent from God.

2 CORINTHIANS 2:12-17

JULIA RECORDED AS PRISCA CONTINUED: "To say that Paulus had a tumultuous relationship with the Christus followers in Corinth is to put things mildly. No congregation was more spiritually gifted, and no congregation was more trouble and aggravation. Because the local leadership was inadequate in Corinth, despite Stephanus and Crispus's best efforts, Paulus had to keep writing them. I know of at least four letters he wrote to Corinth, but there may have been even more.[1] Paulus ultimately knew, however, that he wasn't going to solve all their problems by letters. During his two and a half years in Ephesus he'd already made one return trip to Corinth, only to be rebuffed and deeply hurt by some of the Corinthian Christus followers there, which caused a quick exit and return to Ephesus."

"Were you surprised to see him back so soon?"

"We were! We spent many hours discussing what to do about Corinth. He dispatched both Timothy and Titus to deal with them, also to no avail."

"What eventually happened to the church in Corinth?"

"At the time it looked bleak, but almost five years later, when we met Paulus again in Roma, he told us about a fourth letter to them, which was in some respects a letter of gratitude. He felt they no longer needed 'the rod of discipline.'"

"Was Paulus glad to be back in Ephesus, or was he too distracted about the trouble in Corinth?"

---

[1]See 1 Corinthians 5:9 for reference to Corinthians A; 1 Corinthians=Corinthians B; 2 Corinthians 2:1-4 refers to Corinthians C; and 2 Corinthians=Corinthians D.

"Oh, he was delighted to be back in Ephesus. Paulus called Epaenetus his beloved and the first fruits of Asia.[2] What he meant was *his* first convert in Ephesus. The good news arrived before Paulus ever got there. Indeed, John the elder, the man called the Beloved Disciple whose personal name was Eliezer, had been there. And John also brought Mary, Jesus' mother, because he looked after her. However, before Paulus came and preached to the Gentiles, the converts were almost entirely comprised of Jewish followers of Jesus, since Jews were preaching to fellow Jews."

"How big is Ephesus?"

"It's the largest city in the province of Asia, a bit larger than Corinth, with perhaps fifty-five thousand or so residents, and a lot of visitors, especially at festival times.[3]

"Because of that, this Jewish Christus follower community spawned other assemblies in six cities along the Roman road heading north and east out of Ephesus—assemblies in Smyrna, Pergamum, Thyatira, Sardis, Philadelphia, and finally Laodicea, which is in the Lycus valley and just beyond the province of Asia. I've heard that John, now exiled at Patmos, recently wrote a vast document of apocalyptic prophecy and exhortation to these assemblies, but I've not seen it. The document hasn't reached Roma yet, but the addressees of it, the small communities on the main Roman road out of Ephesus, show us that by and large Paulus didn't attempt to plant fledgling communities where other Christus followers had already done so.[4] The exception was in places where Peter and his co-workers focused on converting Jews. Then Paulus and his coworkers might go to the same

---

[2]Romans 16:5.

[3]The famous theater in Ephesus would hold about twenty-five thousand. Some have suggested that we multiply that seating capacity by ten to get the local population. There is good reason to doubt this. People came to festivals and games in Ephesus from afar, and so the theater was probably larger than needed for just the locals.

[4]Romans 15:20: "It has always been my ambition to preach the gospel where Christ was *not* known, so that I would *not* be building on someone else's foundation" (emphasis added).

place to convert Gentiles. Of course, there were plenty of both in the major cities of the empire."

"Can you give me an example of where that happened?"

"Let's see . . . Peter wrote to his converts in Galatia and Asia,[5] but Paulus also addressed Christus followers in the Lycus valley, but focused more on Colossae than on Laodicea.[6] The division of labor between the apostles wasn't geographical but rather ethnic: Peter, Jacob, and the Beloved Disciple to the circumcised, Paulus and coworkers to the uncircumcised.[7] These were parallel missions, and we prayed for and supported each other in various ways, serving the same Lord. Still, there were more Jewish-flavored communities and more Gentile-flavored ones, depending on which apostle helped plant or grow which group."

"Was this ever a problem?"

Prisca thought a moment. When she answered, she seemed hesitant. "Sometimes circumstances exacerbated the differences between the Jewish and Gentile groups. That was certainly the case in Roma. Aquila and I had no idea what the state of believers would be when we returned to Roma some fourteen years after we had to leave. What we found, however, did not surprise us—the Jewish believers were not meeting with those Gentiles who believed, almost ever, in part because of Claudius's ban. They were afraid of guilt by association I suppose."

"When did you finally return to Roma?"

"In the fall of our third year in Ephesus, we got the good news that Claudius was dead, making all his singular decrees obsolete. Aquila and I spent some two months shoring up the Pauline community in Ephesus, with the promise from Paulus that at some juncture he would send Timothy to

---

[5]1 Peter 1:1-3.
[6]Though see Colossians 4:16. The authentic letter to the Laodiceans is lost, but some ingenious second-century Christian wrote such a document in Paul's name.
[7]Galatians 2:9.

help lead them. Unfortunately, this didn't happen until almost seven or more years later. But still God was gracious, and the community we helped nurture and build continued to grow, a salutary reminder of what the Scriptures say: unless the Lord builds your house, vainly you labor."[8]

Julia perked up at this. "How true. Human beings make all these plans and proposals, but only God makes things happen. It seems that things rarely work out exactly as we think they will."

Prisca smiled. "Indeed! Or as Paulus used to say about the assembly in Corinth, 'I planted the seed, Apollos watered it, but God has been making it grow.'"[9]

Julia started to ask another question, but Prisca stood up and held out her hand, palm forward. "If we get on this subject, we'll be here all day. But I'm famished, so let's save the next portion of the story for the morning."

---

[8]Psalm 127:1.
[9]1 Corinthians 3:6.

13

THE DEATH OF CLAUDIUS, THE RETURN TO ROMA

"Veneno Tiberio Claudio principi per hanc occasionem ab coniuge Agrippino dato."

PLINY, *NATURAL HISTORY* 22.92

JUVENAL, *SATIRE* 5.147

THE NEXT MORNING, FRESHENED BY A DEEP SLEEP, Prisca arose eager to continue her story. Confiding her memories to her daughter's care seemed to be giving her a new energy, a new mission from God that she wanted to see faithfully through, regardless of what any earthly authority might have in store for her. Julia barely had time to get her tablet perched on her lap before Prisca started in again.

"Julia, remember what I said about Paulus's *ethos* problems due to his appearance?"

"Yes. He had eye problems?"

Quotations from Natural History *and* Satire: That is, Agrippina did away with her husband Claudius, says Pliny. Juvenal says it was by a noble *boleti*—that is, a mushroom.

"Right. Well, Claudius had even worse *ethos* problems. He had physical disabilities from an early age—deformities that repelled even some members of his own family. No one ever expected him to become emperor."

Julia had to admit a morbid curiosity. "What do you mean?"

"For instance, when Claudius came of age and put on the *toga virilis*, he was taken for the ceremony at night so that few would see him. And when he was sixteen and went to a gladiatorial spectacle in memory of his father, Drusus, Augustus required him to wear a cloak *over his head*, so he wouldn't distract people! Despite this, and despite a bit of a stutter, Claudius was a bright man who simply didn't look the part of emperor.

"In fact, he was something of a scroll collector. He became a bit of an expert in Roman history and agreed with Augustus when it came to traditional Roman customs and values, which partly explains his allergic reaction to all things Jewish. Had not Germanicus died prematurely and Caligula gone quite mad, Claudius might never have become emperor. He would have been happier just enjoying his scrolls."

"With his odd appearance, did he ever marry?"

"Yes. Power and influence can do what appearance cannot. Claudius married several times, and our fellow believers in Caesar's household told us his last wife, Agrippina, seems to have helped do away with him, probably through poisoned mushrooms. Agrippina made sure it was her own son, and Claudius's stepson, Nero, who became emperor after him—rather than Claudius's own son Britannicus, by his third wife, Messalina. In any case, he was dead just before the Ides of Octobris, which amazingly enough happened on the same day as Aquila's birthday. We celebrated his birthday twice when we later got that news in Ephesus. By then it was far too late to sail to Roma, so we had to wait for the safer Ides of Martius."

"How did you feel about returning to Roma?"

Prisca rose to walk around the room, reflecting on that. "We were full of anticipation but also trepidation about going home to Roma. It was a fine

April day when we returned, not knowing what to expect when we got there. We hadn't heard from our housekeeper Livia the entire time we were gone. Though she was only thirty when we left, by the time we returned she was forty-five. I don't blame Livia for not writing. She was illiterate and hiring a scribe was too expensive." Prisca stopped in front of Julia and added, "I'm so thankful to have you here with me, writing this story, asking such good questions to be sure it's all told."

Julia looked up, a faint smile on her face that Prisca returned. Then she walked to the window, looked out over the garden, and continued her tale, seeing their trek back to Rome once more in her mind's eye. "As we climbed the hill to the *subura* where we then lived, I saw some familiar sights, although several shops seemed to have disappeared to make room for a broader thoroughfare through the *subura.* Fortunately, our *insula* was recognizable and still standing!

"Aquila was so eager to see our place, he raced ahead and took the steps two by two to the second floor and banged on the door of our apartment. A black-haired woman with streaks of gray came to the door, barely cracked it, and said, 'Who's there?'

"'Aquila and Prisca have come home!' he practically roared, and the next thing he knew the woman had fallen on her knees, weeping. When our Livia finally stood and gave us many hugs and holy kisses, she said, 'I thought to never see you again, but when the emperor suddenly died, I thought, Maybe, God willing, there is a chance. But I put it out of my mind as a vain hope, and yet . . . here you are!'

"Standing up, she added, 'And look at you two. The fates have been kind to you. You look older of course, but well.'

"And then I remembered I had left the porter we hired in Puteoli standing in the square below, sweating and cursing his load! I ran down and paid the man, giving him some extra *denarii* for his trouble, and we began to cart our few belongings upstairs, situating them in the little space we had.

"Once we'd settled in, Aquila asked, 'What news in Roma these days?'

"'As you no doubt know, we have a new, young emperor,' Livia said. Then she whispered, 'Fat-faced Nero, such a contrast with Claudius, his stepfather. He doesn't seem much interested in governing, so he's left the job to Seneca, the famous Stoic and rhetorician, and so far, things have gone well. Nero's out attending plays by Euripides or Aristophanes, and playing his lyre, and no one seems to mind. Afranius Burrus is handling all things military and foreign, and Seneca is handling all things domestic, and honestly, I've never seen things run this smoothly in my lifetime.'

"'This is good news indeed,' Aquila said, a little surprised. 'Perhaps we'll have a sunnier political season for a while. But what about our fellow believers in Christus?'

"Livia visibly wilted. 'We've survived in small numbers, but we've not thrived as Jewish followers of Jesus. Our numbers have dwindled while the Gentile believers have increased some. But we lack local leadership. I think we need to do some things together. Perhaps you heard about son of Zebedee Jacob's death at Herod Agrippa's hands? It happened a few years after you were banished.'

"'Yes,' Aquila said solemnly, 'the news reached us in Corinth. The Jerusalem community has had it rough, but then Jesus predicted the sons of Zebedee would suffer martyrdom. "Baptized with the same baptism," he called it. Any news of Peter?'

"'Only that he hasn't come here, yet.'

"Julia, this conversation went on for some time, and I've just summarized what I could remember of it, but overall it was a great day. We had no idea we would never leave Roma again. But Paulus was happy to have us here, to help lay the groundwork for him to come. We knew he would return to Jerusalem first to deliver the collection for the poor.[1] Luke now was Paulus's

---

[1]Acts 20:4.

constant companion, because Paulus needed a constant physician. He'd taken too many beatings over the years, both by Roman rods and by the whip used by the synagogue leader, administering the thirty-nine lashes."[2]

Julia shivered at the thought of such a beating, and Prisca noticed the effect of her words, so she moved ahead in the story.

"When we got home, we went back to our tasks of making tents and began to spread the word that Paulus was coming in due course. In the second year of Nero's reign, there was great excitement because Phoebe of Cenchreae showed up here in Roma, carrying a long letter by Paulus, which he'd written from her house. It was mainly to the majority Gentile congregations in Roma, but of course they shared it with us as well. Apparently, Paulus had good sources as to what was happening to the assemblies of God here in Roma. On the one hand, he never used the word he normally used, *ekklēsia*, or 'assembly', to refer to the whole group of believers here in Roma— not surprisingly, because we never met together. He did refer to us—the little group which, when the letter came, had been meeting for a while in our apartment here, some twenty of us packed into one large room like sardines." Prisca narrowed her shoulders and tried to look squished as she said this, which made Julia chuckle.

"Paulus had actually written a separate letter of introduction and commendation for Phoebe, which included greetings to all of the Jewish Christus followers here in the city and to the God fearers like me who met with them, but what an odd greeting it was. At first, I couldn't make sense of it. Normally, there would be greetings *from* Paulus and those with him, and greetings *to* all those in a city who believed. But in this letter, Paulus asked one group of believers in Roma to embrace and show every sort of affection to another—in this case, he exhorted the Gentiles to embrace their Jewish brothers and sisters. When it finally dawned on me what he was doing, it

---

[2] 2 Corinthians 11:24—five times with the lashes, three times with the rods.

made me cry. He wanted us to start making genuine efforts to be one body in Roma, to meet together from time to time and get to know each other. He wanted us to be more united, and he wanted the Gentile believers to get over their prejudices against the Jewish believers and start heading in a more unified direction when he got here. Julia, will you get me that little document he wrote to this effect? It came with the much longer discourse largely addressing the Gentile believers."

Julia had to rummage around a bit to find the short scroll, but soon enough she brought it back into the garden, where they were composing the chronicle.

"If you don't mind, read out the first portion of this little document of greetings until I say halt."

"Certainly, Domina. I know you have your reasons, so here we go." Julia stood up, assumed a pose like a rhetor, one hand extended toward Prisca for dramatic effect, which made Prisca laugh.

"Perhaps you will become the first female Cicero."

"I think not!" said Julia with a grin, but then she cleared her throat and began reading.[3]

When she finished, Prisca said, "Such a lot of names! I know it was a bit tedious to read them all, but I wanted you to see what I was talking about. First, almost every person listed met with the Jewish believers in Christus. Paulus made sure all the Jewish Christus followers were named and embraced by the Gentile majority. What a clever rhetorical tactic and list of greetings that proved to be.

"Second, notice how many women Paulus names as working for the Lord, including Junia, whom I must say more about in due course. And did you notice the greeting from our friend Erastus?"

Julia nodded.

---

[3]Romans 16.

"Third, notice that near the end, the scribe himself, also a follower of Christus named Tertius, sends greetings. I've never seen that in a letter before, but then I realized this was a separate document commending Phoebe to the Roman believers, followed by many greetings. Paulus had such a wonderful and remarkable memory for names.

"Fourth, notice that Aquila and I are commended for risking our necks for Paulus. He's talking about our adventures in Ephesus and Corinth no doubt—a trial in one city, a riot in another, with us whisking him out of town at the last minute in Ephesus. There seemed to always be an air of danger when Paulus was around.

"Last, notice the strong warning against divisions that plagued us here. Paulus hoped we would start the healing process before he arrived. He had no idea it would take him almost three years to get here! Meanwhile we had much work to do."

Prisca fell silent, so Julia chimed in. "You were going to tell me more about Junia?"

"Let's save that for the morning." Then she added, looking bright, "We're making good progress with this."

"Yes, Domina, but you know the month is slipping away, and that soldier will be returning."

"Don't remind me! I'd almost managed to forget that fact."

14

JOANNA/JUNIA

The women who had come with Jesus from Galilee followed Joseph and saw the tomb and how his body was laid in it. Then they went home and prepared spices and perfumes. But they rested on the Sabbath in obedience to the commandment.

LUKE 23:55-56

When they came back from the tomb, they told all these things to the Eleven and to all the others. It was Mary Magdalene, Joanna, Mary the mother of James, and the others with them who told this to the apostles. But they did not believe the women, because their words seemed to them like nonsense. Peter, however, got up and ran to the tomb.

LUKE 24:9-12

PRISCA AND JULIA WERE UP EARLY, as the days were shortening and becoming cooler. The Ides of Septem would soon be upon them, and it was seen—like the Ides of Martius—as a day of bad luck in Roma. They listened to the city awakening as they ate a light breakfast of fruit and warm, mulled wine.

After swallowing her last bite, Prisca said, "Let's just work here this morning so we won't get in the way of the hired cleaning women."

Julia nodded and picked up her writing tools. Her hand felt cramped from all the writing she'd been doing, so she twirled her wrist and wiggled her fingers, trying to loosen them up as Prisca cleared her throat to begin.

"Women were last at the cross, first at Jesus' tomb, first to see the risen Jesus, and first to proclaim his resurrection, but they were mostly ignored. The men had to find out for themselves. They thought the women were hallucinating or too flighty of mind or too emotional to report accurately what they saw. But one of these women came right here to Roma and bore witness, and you have already read her name."

"Junia," Julia said with satisfaction that they were finally getting to this esteemed person.

"Yes indeed. Remarkably few persons spanned both the ministry of Jesus and made a notable contribution to the life of the growing Jesus movement, but Junia was one of them, and Paulus calls her notable among the apostles. But I want to tell you her whole story, as I knew her personally."

"You've known the most remarkable people!"

"I have indeed. Let's see, where was I . . . oh yes, first things first. The name Joanna is a Hebrew name, and when it's rendered into Latin, it's Junia. In other words, it's the same name with a slight linguistic variation, and the Joanna of the good news account of Luke is the same person as this Junia whom Paulus mentions in his letter to the Romans.

"Even if I didn't know her, I would have been able to figure this out from Paulus's writings. First, he tells us she is a Jew. Second, he says she was 'in Christus before me,' which means she was a Christus follower in the very first years of the movement. Third, she and her husband, Andronicus, were 'in chains' with Paulus. Now, it takes a lot in our male-dominated world for a woman to be placed in chains. She has to have done something truly shocking in public to end up in that sort of fix."

Julia looked alarmed. "What on earth did they do?"

Prisca looked smug and said in a monotone, "They proclaimed the good news about a crucified and risen Jew who was the savior of the world and Lord of all, not to be confused with the claims by the emperor to be the same thing."

"Ah." Julia couldn't help but smirk at that tongue-in-cheek statement. "Where did this happen?"

"In Paulus's hometown of Cilicia in Tarsus." Prisca shook her head. "It did not go well. In Paulus's case, it was another example of what the Lord said. 'A prophet is not without honor except in his own town.'[1] And so, Paulus writes no letters to the believers in Tarsus."

"Was that unusual? Did Paulus always have success?"

"Interesting question, Julia. That's not often mentioned about Paulus' ministry. He had many unsuccessful attempts before successes. Indeed, Paulus got in trouble from the start when he went away to Arabia to try out his message about Jesus, whom he had seen on the road to Damascus. In fact, because of this message, the *ethnarch*[2] of King Aretas of Nabatea pursued Paulus all the way back to Damascus![3]

"Anyway, back to Andronicus and Junia, who were noteworthy among the apostles." That statement gave Prisca pause. "By the way, when Paulus used the word *apostle*, unless he modified it by the phrase 'of the assembly,' as in Antioch, he did not mean an ordinary 'sent one' or messenger or missionary of a Christian assembly. He meant an apostle of Jesus Christus, commissioned by the risen Christus himself, and that only went on during the period when Jesus appeared to people, Paulus being the last to see the risen Lord. In other words, that kind of apostle needs to have seen the risen Lord."[4]

---

[1]Mark 6:4.
[2]An *ethnarch* was a high official, in this case a regional governor under a king, here King Aretas IV.
[3]2 Corinthians 11:32-33.
[4]1 Corinthians 9:1.

"Wait. Before you go any further, I'm confused about something. I thought Joanna of Luke's account was married to a man named Chuza and lived in Galilee on Herod's estate. How could she be married to a man named Andronicus, which is not really a proper Latin name; it's more of a nickname for a 'manly man' from *Andros*. Isn't that right?"

"Excellent question, Julia. Very perceptive of you. Joanna was indeed married to Chuza, Herod Antipas's estate agent, as Luke says in his narrative. She was a high-status woman who became a patroness of Jesus and the Twelve and the female disciples who travelled with him. But as you know, Herod despised John the Baptizer and had him beheaded. And he feared Jesus was John back from the dead when Jesus began his remarkable miracle-working ministry. So Herod told Chuza he must choose. He could rein in his wife and command her to stop travelling around with that prophet from Nazareth, or he could divorce his wife—and if he did not choose one of those two options, he would be out of a lucrative job!

"Chuza chose the path of least resistance and divorced Joanna when she came home from a journey to Nazareth with Jesus' traveling disciples. He simply handed her a writ of divorce and dismissed her."

"Coward!" Julia looked indignant, wanting to defend all women everywhere who were often disposable.

"He certainly was. Joanna, however, was a woman of independent means, so she took her dowry with her and continued to support the Jesus movement. She went with Jesus and the other inner circle of women like Miriam of Magdala to Jerusalem during the last week of Jesus' life, and saw him die a horrible death there. But she visited his tomb where she encountered not only angels but the risen Jesus himself!"[5]

---

[5] While Luke's Gospel is the only one to mention Joanna by name and does not tell us the women at the tomb saw the risen Jesus, both Matthew and, independently, John tells us they did (see Matthew 28:9-10 and John 20, noting the use of the term "we don't know where" on the lips of Miriam of Magdala).

"But where does Andronicus come into the picture?"

"Andronicus, like Stephen, was a Hellenist, a Greek-speaking Jew who was part of the synagogue of the Hellenists in Jerusalem with Stephen. Andronicus was converted by Stephen himself and met Joanna after that Passover. That conversion included being part of some five-hundred persons, including Stephen, who saw the risen Lord during the forty days when Jesus was physically present with his disciples. Thus, he too could claim, 'I have seen the risen Lord.' Andronicus's proper name was Simon, but to avoid confusion with the more famous Simon Peter in Jerusalem, he went by his nickname."

"Ah, I see. It's starting to make sense."

Prisca nodded. "Andronicus and Junia married while being part of the earliest Jerusalem community of believers, and they first heard about the changed Saul, Paulus's Hebrew name, when he came to talk to Peter in Jerusalem. The Christus followers in Judaea were afraid of Saul since he previously worked for the Jewish officials, collecting Christus followers, persecuting them, and bringing them to trial in Jerusalem. Even Andronicus hesitated to work with Paulus, because Saul had been present at and sanctioned Stephen's stoning, before his conversion.[6] But Peter and Jacob convinced Joanna and Andronicus it would be all right to go with Saul to Cilicia and work with him there. Thus began a remarkable partnership with Paulus, like the one Aquila and I had.

"But that's not the end of the story. Paulus wanted all the help he could muster to break down the barriers between the Jewish and Gentile followers of Jesus in Roma."

"What exactly were those barriers?"

"Many Jewish believers remained true to Torah in regard to food, days of worship, and the like, and felt the Gentile followers of Jesus should be more attentive to certain things."

---

[6]See Galatians 1:18-23 on Paul's visit with Peter, and Acts 7–8:1 on Saul and Stephen.

"Such as?"

"For instance, their penchant for eating meat even if it had been sacrificed to idols."

"Was the problem all on the Jewish side?"

"Oh no. The Gentile followers needed to drop their prejudices against Jews as well, so reconciliation in Christus could happen among the believers in Roma.[7]

"They'd been working on this for almost a decade, praying that Paulus would arrive and work some miracles of healed relationships among brothers and sisters in Christus. But, alas, when Paulus wrote to the Romans, he was still almost three full years from getting here. First, he had to go to Jerusalem with the collection, and that proved to be a dangerous and diverting trip in many ways, but we will turn to that tomorrow. For tonight, I have a surprise."

Julia looked up expectantly, raising her eyebrows. "I always like good surprises."

"We are going to have dinner with Junia's daughter, who still lives here in Roma. Her name is Susanna, after Joanna's old friend from Galilee who was also an early disciple of Jesus. We'll hear more of that tonight! But one last thing. Joanna, or Junia, was the female equivalent of Peter, bridging Jesus' ministry and his movement after Pentecost. Actually, she's done more than Peter was able to do here in Roma. But we'll talk about Peter another time."

And so the two women dressed up for an early evening out and headed for the Aventine Hill, where Susanna lived. Dinner tended to be before sundown, as Roma's streets were dangerous at night, and they also took Achilles with them for protection. They were glad to be walking because dinner, called a *cena*, tended to be fulsome, in contrast to the light midday meal.

Susanna's villa was quite small, smaller than Prisca's, and the meal would not be elaborate. Her *triclinium* was only big enough for six to dine. *Triclinium* literally means three couches, and that was all that Susanna's room

---

[7]Romans 14.

could manage, and so each woman had her own. Achilles would eat with the other household staff to allow the three women time alone to talk and enjoy each other's company. The room opened onto a nice view of the garden, which allowed a little breeze into the dining area.

After the usual greetings and procession to the *triclinium,* Susanna said, "We are having some fresh fish this evening, turbot, caught in the Lucrine lake, and some oysters, and of course the usual vegetables, fruits and nuts, and bread and *garum*—and also, some nice olive oil for dipping. I couldn't manage to get the Falernian wine I wanted, so I got the next best thing."

Prisca leaned to pat Susanna on the arm. "It wasn't necessary to do something elaborate, old friend. Julia and I have simple tastes. This will be more than enough, and more than we usually eat."[8]

Susanna relaxed at this reassurance. "Oh, but we will eat in a leisurely manner, for I have some stories my mother told me about when she traveled with Jesus during his ministry."

Prisca's face lit up at this news. "Excellent! I want to know more about that whole period of time and what the first disciples were like, and since Julia has brought her wax tablet along, she'll take some notes, as we are in the process of writing up a chronicle of the movement of Christus followers in our time."

"Wonderful!" Susanna clearly felt honored to be included in Prisca's tale. "Where shall I begin? Perhaps with the story mother told me, which she heard personally from Miriam of Magdala, about how she came to be a follower of Jesus." Suddenly, concern clouded her brow. "The story is somewhat disturbing. Shall I tell it?"

---

[8]See Angelo Angela, *A Day in the Life of Ancient Rome* (New York: Europa Editions, 2009), 271. Angela is able to estimate the cost of various items based on the records from the time of Trajan. For example, one quart of olive oil equals three sestertii equals $7.50; one bottle of table wine equals one sestertius equals $2.50; one loaf of bread equals one-half sestertius equals $1.25; and one really good-sized fish would be about $5.00. For a person of average means, a banquet would be an expensive proposition, only indulged in rarely.

Julia nodded. "Please do. My mistress has toughened me up so that I have a rather good capacity for listening to disturbing stories without being put off my food."

Susanna and Prisca looked at each other and chuckled.

"Very well, then." Susanna moved to the edge of her seat and put her hands together, signaling she was about it begin.

"On the northwest corner of the sea called Kinneret or Tiberias sat the village of Migdal (Magdala), between Kefer-Nahum (Capernaum) and Bet-saida (Bethsaida).[9] All three of these villages were fishing villages, and business was booming. One could always tell when things were going well— more tax collectors would show up to take their cut for Herod."

This brought wide eyes and a knowing nod from Prisca.

"The people of Magdala however weren't grumbling about tax collectors as they usually did, as there was a new topic of conversation—the beautiful new synagogue in Magdala, complete with a stone reading table decorated with floral designs and a carved image of a menorah. The pride in the little village was palpable since the synagogue had been completed earlier in the summer.

"High above the fishing village in the hills that led to the cliffs of Arbel was a cave, and sitting in its mouth a woman, covered in dust from head to toe. She was not an old woman, but it was clear life had not been kind to her. She had no one to talk to.

"'Unclean,' they say. 'But who are they, the lords of life, to judge

Figure 14.1. A limestone Torah table with a menorah carved in the side.

[9]This material is adapted from Ben Witherington III, *The Gospel of Jesus: A True Story* (Seedbed Publishing, 2014), 43-45.

me?' she asked no one in particular. Her hair disheveled, she'd covered herself in dirt to protect herself from the relentless sun but also the vermin that crawled around the cave. Her name was Miryam (Mary), named for the prophetess, the sister of Moses. But she was not honored among men like Miryam in the Torah. No, indeed she had been cast out of the village because they suspected she had unclean spirits. Stories drifted down that hillside that if men tried to use her for their pleasure, she thwarted them. Despite her small frame she had a loud, ferocious voice when she wanted to use it, and she defended herself with shrieks and kicks, fighting them off. Her parents were dead and her only brother had left town looking for work elsewhere, leaving her well and truly alone. Miryam was just twenty-five when she came to this cave.

"Seeking help and cleansing from God, she tried to enter the new synagogue early on Shabbat, but suddenly, as had happened before, she blacked out, fell down, began to writhe on the new mosaic floor as spittle foamed from her mouth. The president in charge of maintenance of the new synagogue called for several townsmen to help him drag her out of the holy place, as clearly she was unclean and might even be possessed by demons.

"Miryam awoke some time later lying just beyond the graveyard, just beyond the town boundary stone. Bruised from the fall, bewildered as to why she was there, she saw a tall olive-skinned man with dark hair, the watchman and caretaker of the graveyard, who told her, 'You cannot come into the town or synagogue again. You are possessed, unclean, unwell, cursed by God. We cannot have you contaminating others in our village, much less contaminating the holy place. Here is your bundle of clothes and things. Take them and go away—anywhere but Magdala. You are not welcome here ever again!' and he pushed her up the hill so that she stumbled.

"Reeling from the events of the day, Miryam wandered up the hill to where the shepherds and sheep were. She found a little cave, where she now sat. In her more lucid moments, she'd asked the shepherds where the spring water

was, and she'd found some abandoned olive and fig trees to provide food. In exchange for sewing garments for the itinerant shepherds and goatherds, Miryam traded for bread as well. But apart from this sporadic contact with humankind, she lived alone. The spider and the scorpion, the birds, and the wild animals, were her only regular companions. Cast out, cast down, casting about for food and life, she lived in maddening and utter isolation.

"Shortly after this. Jesus came over the final hill above the Kinneret.[10] As he headed down the slope to the beautiful lake below, he saw someone sitting alone by the spring that came from the limestone cliffs above. She eagerly gulped water, and washed her hands and face over and over again. Parched from the long walk, Jesus decided to stop for a drink as well, and to fill up his wineskin for the next stage of the journey.

"When Jesus came near the spring, the woman began shrieking at the top of her voice, recoiling in horror as Jesus approached. Suddenly in an inhumanly loud voice she said, 'Do not torment me son of David. Have mercy upon me!'

"The woman's face contorted out of all recognition, and she shook all over. Spittle drooled down the right side of her mouth. Holding his right hand out toward the woman, Jesus felt a surge of power race through his body, and then he said in a stern tone of voice, 'Leave her! Now! And never return again! In the name of the Almighty I cast you out!' The woman gave another ear-splitting scream, convulsed and rolled on the ground. After a long silence Jesus said, 'Shalom to you, may God's wholeness now prevail in your life.'

"At first the woman stared into the distance, as if she was not even present, and then the tears quietly streamed down her face.

"'What is your name, daughter of Abraham?'

"Her feeble voice barely croaked, 'Miryam, Miryam of Migdal.'

---

[10]Adapted from Witherington, *The Gospel of Jesus.*

"After sitting with her for a few minutes until she caught her breath and recovered her bearings, Jesus said, 'Come daughter of Abraham, let us go down to your village below, and I will vouch to the local elder or priest that you are once more in your right mind.' Handing her his walking stick, as she was still shaky and wobbly, this odd pair headed to the village below.

"This was actually how Jesus' ministry started."

"Truly?" Julia asked in surprise.

"Yes, Jesus had two or three male disciples with him at the wedding feast at Cana, but the Twelve were not yet assembled, and Peter was not yet the leader of the male disciples, as Miryam was to become of the female disciples. And that group of female disciples—Miryam, my mother, Susanna, for whom I am named, and various others—were as loyal to Jesus as the male disciples, indeed more so at the end when the men abandoned, denied, or betrayed him. These women traveled with Jesus all over Galilee, and my mother, in particular, supported all of them out of her own funds when there was no hospitality to be had in one village or another in Galilee, and then in Judaea as well."

"What they must have seen!" Julia marveled.

"Oh my, yes. These women saw many miracles, along with Jesus and the male disciples, and listened to Jesus' teaching. Miryam became an important source for Luke when he wrote his account of Jesus."

"When was that?"

"During the two years of Paulus's incarceration in Caesarea Maritima. By then Miryam was an old woman, but she still had a crystal-clear memory of her traveling days with Jesus. In particular, she shared some wonderful parables that only Luke recounts: of the Good Samaritan, of the Pharisee and the tax collector, of the wayward son who returned, of the rich man and Lazarus. Luke was a good storyteller, but he owed these tales to Miryam's vivid memory. And Miryam was the first to see our risen Lord once he was raised from death, but that's a story for another day."

The women enjoyed each other's company for a couple of hours, and then Achilles appeared in the opening from the garden and said, "Domina, the sun is setting. We need to begin our journey home."

The women rose, embraced each other, and gave the traditional holy kiss in saying their farewells. Julia chatted excitedly all the way home. She would have continued into the wee hours of the night, but Prisca made it clear she was retiring. Tomorrow would be upon them before they knew it, and time was precious right now.

15

PAULUS'S FAREWELL AT MILETUS

Only in the agony of parting do we look into the depths of love.

George Eliot

The month nearly gone, Julia dreaded the knock on the door surely to come soon. But she tried not to dwell on it or to say anything to Prisca. It seemed better at the moment to dwell on the past, or the glorious future promised to come, rather than on the present. So she pushed her anxious thoughts aside and brought Prisca a warm drink and a small tray of sweet grapes from the vineyards just outside the city walls, knowing the grapes were the perfect ripeness, which would bring Prisca delight.

"Thank you, dear one. You are kind to me." Prisca popped a grape in her mouth and savored the sweet juices. Her throat was a bit hoarse this morning, but the warm drink helped clear it. As had become their pattern, Prisca began her tale once she had taken some basic refreshment.

"I think Paulus knew that all that opposition in various cities in the empire would eventually catch up with him, but he believed it wouldn't happen before he completed what God wanted him to do. It was dangerous to tell Gentiles not to worship the city gods in Roma or elsewhere, dangerous because all of city life—economic, home, military—was intertwined with its religious life. In all these realms, most assumed they needed the support of the gods, or at least they didn't want the gods as adversaries. So Paulus could see the outlines of the future, but not all the details, as is clear from reading the end of his letter to us who were in Roma, where he says he's coming our way just as soon as he can drop off the collection in Jerusalem."

"What do you mean? What outlines of the future did he see?"

"I'll put it another way, as Daniel put it: Paulus saw the 'handwriting on the wall.'[1] He knew the inevitable outcome of his life, but he didn't know the timing of various things along the way. And this was true in regard to his visit with the Ephesian elders as he was journeying from Troas down the coast to Miletus, and then onto a boat bound for Syria and Jerusalem. He said farewell to them, with tears all around, said he'd never see them again, and yet . . . he did. After he was released from house arrest in Roma, he turned toward Ephesus to deal with problems Timothy couldn't handle. But he avoided stopping in Ephesus, where his riot-causing action was still fresh in the minds of some there, such as the silversmiths like Demetrius who led the attempt to do away with Paulus."

Prisca and Julia sat in the *tablinum,* the business

Figure 15.1. An *impluvium*, or raincatcher, near the front of a house in Pompeii.

---

[1]See Daniel 5.

portion of the house, cooled by a fall rain. Both paused for a moment to watch the rain fall through the hole in the roof into the catch basin, providing fresh rainwater for their home.

"Domina, since he knew the danger, why did Paulus insist on going personally with the collection to Jerusalem? Couldn't he have sent representatives from the assemblies in Macedonia and Greece and Galatia without endangering himself, since he was eager to come here?"

Prisca sighed as if the weight of those bygone days were once again on her shoulders. "He *could* have done that, but he'd heard about the whispers in Jerusalem that he was a renegade Jew who'd abandoned his heritage and had started a new religion for Gentiles. He sincerely wanted the Jewish and Gentile portions of Christus's body to be united, and he wanted the blessing and endorsement of the Jerusalem church, despite saying he didn't really need to have it. He knew that without acceptance of the mother assembly he would be 'running my race in vain,' as he put in his first letter.[2] He deeply believed that in God's eyes, which should also be how we see things, 'in Christus there is neither Jew nor Gentile, neither slave nor free, nor is there male and female, for you are all one in Christus Jesus.'[3] He wasn't naïve enough to think these divisions would cease to exist when one became a Christus follower, but he believed they should not divide us, for we are all created in God's image, all of sacred worth, all being transformed into the image of Christus."

Julia looked wistful. "It's a beautiful vision of a united church."

"It is, and it's what Paulus believed God was in the process of creating. He believed in God's miraculous ability to resurrect things and change people. He fervently believed the promises in Isaiah that one day swords would be beaten into plowshares, one day we would study war no more, one day the wolf would lie down with the lamb, one day disease, decay, death, suffering, sin, and sorrow would be overcome once and for all by God's resurrecting, life-giving power. But he knew ultimately this would not

---

[2]Galatians 2:2.
[3]Galatians 3:28.

happen until Christus returned. Until then, the assembly of God everywhere should reflect this final state of affairs, so Paulus kept placing before us what God ultimately had in mind—-that we love God wholeheartedly, that we love one another the same way, even that we love our enemies and pray for those who persecute us, as Jesus told us to do."

"That's so very hard, and contrary to human nature."

"It is, but Paulus had seen how God in Christus could change human nature by his grace—indeed, he had experienced it in his own life, so he was confident of the final outcome whatever battles remained along the way."

"I wish I had that much confidence, but Domitianus scares me to death," confessed Julia, biting her tongue after her resolve not to speak of the impending terror.

Yet brave Prisca didn't miss a beat. "He scares me too, but I'm putting my hopes in front of my fears, quite deliberately."

"How do you do that?"

"By faith alone. I believe God loves me, that he is more powerful than even Domitianus, and that God can work all things together for good, whether it's a favorable outcome for me or not." She had been looking off into the distance as if in another time and place, but now she smiled and looked directly at Julia. "Ultimately, I will have the most favorable outcome possible."

Something in Prisca's words touched Julia deeply. She brushed away an unexpected tear and sat up a little straighter. "Thank you, Domina. That helps. But it's so very hard."

"It is. I agree. We constantly battle against fear, but it gets easier with much opportunity and practice. You are yet young. I want you to learn to live with hope, not fear."

"I want that too. Pray for me in that regard."

Prisca reached out and patted Julia's knee. "I most certainly will." She kept her hand there, and both fell silent for a few moments until Julia resolved in a businesslike tone, "We must get back to the story."

Prisca nodded, took a sip of wine, popped another grape in her mouth, and continued. "Knowing he would not be with his converts forever, Paulus gradually set up leaders along the way—for instance, the elders in Ephesus, Philippi, and later on, Crete.[4] So it was that he summoned the Ephesian elders to meet him in Miletus, which he'd traveled to on foot from Troas, bypassing Ephesus itself. There he gave a stirring speech, full of pathos and tears. *Everyone* was crying in the end."

Prisca thought a moment. "Paulus was either greatly loved or greatly loathed—no one could ignore him or feel indifferent about him. Julia, let's put Luke's account of that famous speech into our story."

Julia reached into the leather pail with a *capsa*, or lid, that had been made in Prisca's shop. She pulled out the large second chronicle written to Theophilus, scanning it for the speech.

Figure 15.2. *Capsae*, or scroll cases.

"It's about two thirds through the manuscript, give or take a little."

"Aha, I've found it." Julia began to read: "You know how I lived the whole time I was with you, from the first day I came into the province of Asia. I served the Lord with great humility and with tears and in the midst of severe testing by the plots of my Jewish opponents. You know that I have not hesitated to preach anything that would be helpful to you but have taught you publicly and from house to house. I have declared to both Jews and Greeks that they must turn to God in repentance and have faith in our Lord Jesus.

"And now, compelled by the Spirit, I am going to Jerusalem, not knowing what will happen to me there. I only know that in every city the Holy Spirit warns me that prison and hardships are facing me. However, I consider my

---

[4]Philippians 1:1-3; Titus 1.

life worth nothing to me; my only aim is to finish the race and complete the task the Lord Jesus has given me—the task of testifying to the good news of God's grace.

"Now I know that none of you among whom I have gone about preaching the kingdom will ever see me again. Therefore, I declare to you today that I am innocent of the blood of any of you. For I have not hesitated to proclaim to you the whole will of God. Keep watch over yourselves and all the flock of which the Holy Spirit has made you overseers. Be shepherds of the church of God, which he bought with his own blood. I know that after I leave, savage wolves will come in among you and will not spare the flock. Even from your own number men will arise and distort the truth in order to draw away disciples after them. So be on your guard! Remember that for three years I never stopped warning each of you night and day with tears.

"Now I commit you to God and to the word of his grace, which can build you up and give you an inheritance among all those who are sanctified. I have not coveted anyone's silver or gold or clothing. You yourselves know that these hands of mine have supplied my own needs and the needs of my companions. In everything I did, I showed you that by this kind of hard work we must help the weak, remembering the words the Lord Jesus himself said: 'It is more blessed to give than to receive.'

"When Paulus had finished speaking, he knelt down with all of them and prayed. They all wept as they embraced him and kissed him. What grieved them most was his statement that they would never see his face again. Then they accompanied him to the ship."[5]

"Luke summarized Paulus' ministry nicely," Prisca said, "and captured the way he related to his fellow believers. Ironically, it's the only speech Luke records that Paulus gave to followers of Christus. All the other speeches are to officials or the unconverted in general."

---

[5]Acts 20:22-37.

Julia barely heard Prisca as she thought about Luke's document. "Domina, I've wondered over the purpose of this second chronicle written to Theophilus. Why did Luke write it?"

"Excellent question, Julia. You are learning to think in whys instead of whats. I like that. Luke's second document was meant to portray the *beginnings* of the movement as the good news spread from Jerusalem to Roma. It's not a biography of the Twelve or even the apostles. Indeed, it only gives a good deal of ink and papyrus to Peter and Paulus. It's hardly 'the Acts of the Apostles,' as I've heard some call it. Nor is it really about the situations that *followed* the evangelism and planting of congregations here and there. Some have complained that Luke doesn't even mention Paulus's writing letters, but all of his letters are addressed to those who are *already* followers of Christus—whether individuals like Philemon, or Timothy, or Titus, or congregations he founded. In other words, the letters aren't about the *initial* missionary preaching; they're about discipleship, whereas the manuscript you just read from is meant to fill in the gaps about the initial preaching and sowing of the Word. Luke's account is about beginnings. Paulus's letters are about continuing, and the ongoing promise and problems of assemblies here and there."

"Is this why Luke ends his account with Paulus sharing the good news here in Roma but doesn't tell of Paulus's end here in Roma?"

"Yes. Luke was a good Greek historian, only as good as his sources. He had much material from Paulus, and some from others, but his focus was on the spreading movement from Jerusalem to Roma. He didn't encourage a personality cult focused on Paulus or Peter. His focus was on the Word as a change agent, not the human vessels through which it was spoken."

"Could you explain what you mean by that?"

Prisca looked around the room for inspiration and focused on the instrument in Julia's hand. "Imagine this stylus could talk. Imagine that it bragged, 'I have written many great plays for Euripides!' How farcical!

Paulus knew he was merely an instrument in God's hand, spreading the good news. He sowed, but only God could produce a crop. Paulus was a strong leader, but he wasn't an arrogant, self-centered person like many of our rulers. Indeed, he loved to say that Christus had crucified his old self, and now Christus lived in him.[6] He lived as Christus's slave, not for personal gain or fame."

Julia tapped her stylus on her cheek as she listened, then put it down. "I see. That's wonderfully reassuring, given that I'm the instrument you're trusting to help tell this story."

Prisca smiled. "It is indeed! And it's the way we should all look at what we do."

Julia nodded, absorbing this wisdom a few moments more before returning to the task at hand. "I know Paulus took his leave of the Ephesian elders after a tearful reunion and then sailed on to Syria with representatives of various assemblies. What then?"

"What followed was in some ways surprising, in some ways predictable. Indeed, Agabus, a prophet from the Jerusalem assembly, warned Paulus about what would happen. Yet Agabus was only partially right. Perhaps he didn't heed Paulus's warning about prophesying only as far as one's faith. But in any case, the prophecy didn't stop Paulus from fulfilling his mission, as we shall see."

Prisca stood and stretched, listening to the patter of rain and the rumbling of thunder in the distance. "Let's have more fruit and some nuts, and perhaps some warm soup on this rainy day; then we can continue the chronicle once I've rested for an hour or so."

"That sounds wonderful! I'll see to the soup."

---

[6]Galatians 2:19-20.

16

THE COLLECTION AND ITS COLLECTORS REACH JERUSALEM

I shall borrow from Epicurus: "The acquisition of riches has been for many men, not an end, but a change, of troubles." I do not wonder. For the fault is not in the wealth, but in the mind itself. That which had made poverty a burden to us, has made riches also a burden. Just as it matters little whether you lay a sick man on a wooden or on a golden bed, for whithersoever he be moved he will carry his malady with him; so one need not care whether the diseased mind is bestowed upon riches or upon poverty. His malady goes with the man.

SENECA, *MORAL EPISTLES* 1.17

"Whoever does not regard what he has as most ample wealth, is unhappy, though he be master of the whole world."

SENECA, QUOTING EPICURUS, *MORAL EPISTLES* 1.9

THE SUNDIAL IN THE GARDEN CAST a small shadow as the clouds scudded by above, with some weak, intermittent sun peeking through. A sense of dread had settled over Prisca's house, but no one dared mention anything about a soldier knocking on the door. The rest of the household constantly thought of possible consequences if Prisca was taken away for good. Yet Prisca seemed remarkably calm as she and Julia reclined in the *triclinium*. Eventually, they went to the small guest room at the front of the house where they arranged two chairs so they could face each other as Prisca spoke and Julia wrote.

"Jesus and Paulus often warned against loving money. Jesus said you cannot serve the two masters, God and money. And Paulus said loving money is a root of all kinds of evil. Money itself isn't evil; it can even be a blessing from God. But as Seneca says, the fault is not in money; it's in the mind or heart of the individual who has it. Like Seneca, Paulus often shared about contentment."

"I'm confused, Domina. Why are we talking about money?"

"I'm getting to that. I realize I bring up ideas that seem random to you, but my thoughts have a clear direction. Anyway, I want you to understand how remarkable his behavior was in the collection he took for the poor saints in Jerusalem. You must understand the shaky relationship Paulus had with the Jerusalem assembly. Some railed against him and came behind him in Galatia to force Gentiles to become full-fledged Jews in order to be Christus's followers, which the Jerusalem council, headed by Jacob the brother of Jesus, thankfully put an end to.[1] Nevertheless, Paulus determined to help the Jerusalem congregation survive and thrive. And he wanted it to be abundantly clear that the money came from largely Gentile churches. As he was to say in his letter to the Romans, it was simply an attempt to thank that mother congregation for the spiritual blessings received from

---

[1] Galatians 1-4; Acts 15.

the apostles.[2] It was not a polite bribe to leave us alone. It was not an attempt to set up a reciprocity cycle."

"So did the offering accomplish what Paulus hoped?"

"Sadly, it did not. Because of suspicions, Jacob told Paulus to go to the temple and use some of the money to support various Christus followers who had undertaken a Nazaritic vow. When Paulus went to the temple, all Hades broke loose. Paulus was accused of sacrilege, of bringing a Gentile too far into the temple, which was absolutely false. Fortunately, a Roman soldier from the Antonia Fortress rescued him. In hindsight, it was probably unwise to try to speak with the mob in the court of the Gentiles because that just made things worse. He was recognized by some and mistaken for someone worse by others. In any case, Paulus ended up under house arrest in Caesarea, where he sat for almost two years waiting for his case to be resolved. Fortunately, Luke still had access to him, and providentially, this gave Luke time to gain knowledge of the mother assembly in Jerusalem, to meet some of the earliest *Christianoi,* as the Romans call us, 'partisans of Christus' or 'those belonging to Christus,' and to find out the sort of things he writes about in the first third of his second volume. Luke followed the Greek procedure of seeking out and consulting eyewitnesses and the original participants among the followers of Jesus."[3]

"I can see how God used that time for Luke, but it must have been difficult for Paulus."

"Yes! And even worse, when Paulus was put under house arrest in Caesarea Maritima during the reign of Felix and then Festus, not a *single* member of the congregation in Jerusalem came to his aid or defense. Not one! He had to fend for himself, which fortunately he was able to do being a Roman citizen, finally appealing to Roma. I suppose the congregation in Jerusalem was too frightened, trying to lay low, trying not to draw attention to itself.

---

[2]Romans 15.
[3]Luke 1:1-4.

I can partially understand this, since tensions were already rising in Jerusalem, and before too long war between zealous Jews and the authorities would break out all over the country.

"It's interesting how God works. Jesus told Paulus in that first vision that one day he would bear witness before high authorities and kings. What Paulus didn't expect was that it would be during the course of a hearing in Caesarea, when he had a chance to address Herod Agrippa and Bernice as well as the Roman proconsuls. But he looked forward to finally being able to speak to Nero himself. However, things didn't turn out as expected."

Julia was curious. "But why would Paulus simply stay in Caesarea so long, when he could have immediately appealed to Caesar?"

"A wise question. I think Paulus was reluctant to keep the trial process going if he could avoid appealing to Caesar. He must have hoped he could be released in Caesarea and come to Roma a free man. But it was not to be. He came, so to speak, courtesy of the Roman jurisprudence and escort service!"

Julia laughed at this. "So to speak!"

"But Paulus was not afraid. All he cared about was fulfilling his mission. I've never met a person with that much certainty about his calling, and the conviction that he would fulfill it. He had absolute trust that God providentially arranged his circumstances."

Prisca's words hit Julia like a lightning bolt. Surely, God was in control of all circumstances, even if it meant her beloved mentor should have to appear before the highest court in the land. She endeavored to trust as Paulus did.

PAULUS THE PRISONER IN CAESAREA AND THE STRUGGLES OF THE *EKKLĒSIA* IN ROMA

I will first set down the names of the waters which enter the City of Rome; then I will tell by whom, under what consuls, and in what year after the founding of the City each one was brought in; then at what point and at what milestone each water was taken; how far each is carried in a subterranean channel, how far on substructures, how far on arches. Then I will give the elevation of each, [the plan] of the taps, and the distributions that are made from them; how much each aqueduct brings to points outside the City, what proportion to each quarter within the City; how many public reservoirs there are, and from these how much is delivered to public works, how much to ornamental fountains (munera, as the more polite call them), how much to the water-basins; how much is granted in the name of Caesar; how much for private uses by the favour of the Emperor;

what is the law with regard to the construction and maintenance
of the aqueducts, what penalties enforce it, whether established by
resolutions of the Senate or by edicts of the Emperors.

SEXTUS JULIUS FRONTINUS, *THE AQUARIUS OF ROMA*, 1.3

PRISCA PICKED UP HER TALE AS JULIA RECORDED: "We didn't
have any letters from Paulus during his two-year hiatus in Caesarea. He was
certainly wise in turning down the suggestion that he return to Jerusalem
and stand trial there. That sort of thing ended badly for Jesus, Stephen, and
Jacob son of Zebedee, who was executed by Herod Agrippa.

"And indeed, shortly after Paulus sailed from Caesarea to Roma, Jacob
the brother of Jesus was martyred by the grandson of Ananus, the high priest
in Jesus' day. No, Paulus was wise to finally appeal to Caesar. He was not
about to pay a bribe to a proconsul to be released. And if he were in Roman
custody, the Roman authorities would protect him from further mayhem
along the way to Roma."

"Did Luke go with Paulus? And what was happening in Roma at the time?"

Figure 17.1. The Caesarea aqueduct brought fresh water to the city Herod built by the sea.

"Yes, Luke accompanied him, and Paulus was optimistic about Nero's reign. Things were calm, and Paulus instructed us to recognize and submit to the governing authorities and to pay our taxes and honor those who upheld justice.[1] All of this 'calm' I credit to noble Seneca, who was perhaps our best philosopher and knew what it took to govern wisely. We had something of an unclouded day, a few years without trouble. And we began to do as Paulus wished—to meet with the Gentile Christian groups in Roma."

"Was Peter in Roma yet?"

Figure 17.2. The tomb of a merchant named Flavius Zeuxis outside the city gate in Hierapolis.

"No, not at this time. In fact, there were no great apostles in the Eternal City. We had to make do with the local leaders we had."

In light of Prisca's current trouble with Domitianus, Julia kept ruminating on a question that concerned her now. "Explain to me more about what Paulus instructed about how we should respond to the governing authorities."

---

[1]Romans 13:1-7.

Prisca stood and paced a bit, as if the question stirred something deep within her that prevented her from sitting still. "Keep in mind that when Paulus wrote to us in Roma, he assumed the government would operate as it should do, upholding *iustitia,* justice."

"Yes," Julia said, nodding, expecting Prisca to talk about how Nero certainly didn't do that, but Prisca surprised her.

"Julia, today we hear rumbling about Nero—or the so-called third Nero—being the anti-Christus, or the one called 666, because of the persecutions that began to happen under Nero's reign. But this was not the situation here when Paulus wrote his letter to us. Paulus had some pride in being a Roman citizen and in Roman law."

Julia shook her head, confused. "Can you explain to me about those Jewish symbolic numbers? I've never grasped what that's about."

"It's called *gematria,* and certain numbers are crucial; for example, the number seven was considered the number of perfection, whereas the number 666 would indicate that which falls short of perfect, so chaos. Twelve, as in the twelve tribes of Israel or the twelve apostles, and multiples of twelve, such as 144,000, symbolically represent the whole people of God."

Figure 17.3. The inscription from the tomb of Flavius Zeuxis, which reads in part: "Flavius Zeuxis, a man loving hard toil at his trade, engaged in the good business of mariner." It adds that he made thirty-six round trips by sea safely to Roma.

"So how does that work?"

"We use letters of the alphabet for numbers in Hebrew and Greek and Latin, and each letter of the alphabet has a numerical value beginning with the first letter of the alphabet—so *aleph* in Hebrew or *alpha* in Greek equals the number one, and so on.[2]

"Here's the most interesting part. If you look at a silver denarius that has Nero's picture on it, what's the inscription on it?"

Julia fished through the purse tied to the belt around her waist. "This one reads 'NERO CAESAR AVGVSTVS DIVI FILII.'"

"Indeed, it does. Can you guess what the total gematric numerical value of Nero's name is?"

"Umm, I have a feeling you're going to tell me it's 666."

"Not quite. It's actually 616, *but*, in the eastern end of the empire the coins were minted with the Emperor's name reading as NERON, which does add up to 666. In other words, *gematria* was a way to indirectly critique a bad emperor."[3]

Julia shuddered, advising with sarcasm, "I would recommend *not* mentioning that when you are brought before the tribunal of Domitianus in coming days."

"To be sure," Prisca said, laughing, "I shall not bring that up."

---

[2]What we call Arabic numbers seem to have originated in India in the sixth or seventh century AD, introduced to Europe through the writings of Arab mathematicians, especially al-Khwarizmi and al-Kindi, but not until about the twelfth century. Before then Christians used Roman numerals, for example. A very interesting ancient Arab university or school in biblical Haran has an astrological pool and a stargazing tower as well, which is one of the places where modern mathematics began to be practiced, using Arabic numbers.

[3]If one does critical research on Revelations 13:18, one will discover that some texts from the eastern end of the empire have 666—for instance, the Alexandrian text—and some texts from the west have 616.

18

AT LAST! PAULUS'S ARRIVAL IN ROMA

And so we came to Rome. The brothers and sisters there had heard that we were coming, and they traveled as far as the Forum of Appius and the Three Taverns to meet us. At the sight of these people Paul thanked God and was encouraged. When we got to Rome, Paul was allowed to live by himself, with a soldier to guard him.

ACTS 28:14-16

There is no place in town, Sparsus, where a poor man can either think or rest. One cannot live for schoolmasters in the morning, corn grinders at night, and coppersmiths' hammers all day and night. Here the money-changer indolently rattles piles of Nero's rough coins on his dirty counter; there a beater of Spanish gold belabors his worn stone with shining mallet. Nor does the fanatic rabble of Bellona cease from its clamor, nor the chatty sailor with his piece of wreck hung over his shoulder; nor the Jewish boy, brought up to begging by his mother, nor the blear-eyed huckster of matches. Who can enumerate the various interruptions to sleep at Rome? As well might you tell

how many hands in the city strike the cymbals, when the moon under
eclipse is assailed with the magic dance.

MARTIAL, *EPIGRAMS* 12.57

JULIA PROMPTED PRISCA TO CONTINUE HER STORY: "So when did Paulus finally get to Roma?"

"Not until the fifth year of Nero's reign—and only after a shipwreck off the coast of Melita."[1]

"Oh my goodness!" Julia exclaimed. She couldn't imagine the terror of a shipwreck. Being on the sea made her stomach queasy, so she didn't like traveling that way. The idea of the ship going down while she was on it only added to her aversion.

"Oh yes, and that wasn't the first time that had happened to Paulus. Yet he stayed calm during the whole ordeal, actually saving some lives as they were abandoning the ship on the rocks.[2] Paulus was not easily discouraged from finishing the tasks God called him to do."

"I should say not!"

Prisca chuckled. "Back to our story. Fortunately, for eight years while Seneca was Nero's advisor, things went rather smoothly, except of course for Nero's own personal immoral behavior, but don't let me get started on that. I mention this because Paulus arrived and was under house arrest during the last three years of that collaboration and supervision of Nero's reign. Paulus had good reason to expect that as a Roman citizen—and for the fact that the Romans didn't like or listen to complaining Jews—he would survive in the Roman courts. Sadly, Seneca like Socrates took his own life the year after the great fire in Roma, when he was falsely accused of plotting to have

---

[1] Melita is the Greek name from which Malta comes.
[2] 2 Corinthians 11:25 says he was shipwrecked three times before that journey to Rome!

Nero killed, as if he would stoop to be part of the Pisonian conspiracy.[3] But it was all a lie."

That statement seemed to take something out of Prisca. "I'll tell you more about that tomorrow morning, but for now I need some rest."

Julia happily put everything down and stretched. "Yes, Domina, this cold, rainy weather makes me want to sleep even more than normal and to stay inside. We'll continue this afternoon."

But in the afternoon after a brief rest, instead of continuing, Prisca and Julia decided to walk down into the *subura* so they could see how the work was going in Prisca's leather-workers' shop. Before arriving, they strolled down the street of scroll sellers in the *Argiletum*, and Julia and Prisca decided to make a stop at their friend Julius's shop. In spite of being elderly, short, and balding, Julius always managed to make his customers smile. He enthusiastically greeted Prisca and Julia, waving them over to see an exciting new advancement over the ordinary scroll.

Figure 18.1 and figure 18.2. Older papyrus compared to a much later example of a biblical text inscribed on parchment in four columns.

"I'm telling you, the codex is the wave of the future," Julius said. "So much easier to handle, you don't have to carry multiple scrolls around of longer works. It's all compact and even sewn together. Of course,

---

[3] The conspiracy of Gaius Calpurnius Piso in AD 65, in which Piso sought to have Nero assassinated, was a major turning point in the reign of Nero. The plot arose because of the serious discontent among the ruling class of the Roman state with Nero's increasingly dictatorial leadership.

the cheaper ones still use papyrus, but now we have a copy of Homer's *Odyssey* in the Greek on parchment, which will never tear or crumple or fade.[4] I mean, compare it to this very old copy of the *Odyssey*." He carefully unrolled a fragile, yellowed scroll for the women to see and continued, "And here it is on parchment. See how much clearer the writing is, and how the surface holds the ink and keeps its distinctness without fading!"

"Yes," said Prisca, "there is a world of difference, and I'm imagining a world of difference in price too!"

"Well, for quality," said Julius winking at Prisca, "you always have to be prepared to pay a bit more, but for you, I have a special deal this morning. I need a new pair of good sandals, and a satchel to carry things in. Can we barter? I'll give you the manuscript in exchange for those two small items."

Prisca gave him a wry look. "You've not lost your touch, and I'm betting you're coming out on the plus side of the ledger on this deal." She clapped her hands together once and said, "But as it happens, I need a new copy of Homer's classic work. Julia's ancient Greek is getting a little rusty, and besides, it's a grand story. Indeed, it's the basis for our own classic, Virgil's *Aeneid*."

Julia peeked over Prisca's shoulder and asked, "When was that written?"

"When Augustus came to power," Prisca answered. To Julius she said, "I'll have someone from the shop bring the items right over, and Julia, will you relieve Julius of his fine codex. This will provide us enjoyable reading in the evenings before we turn in."

The codex was rather heavy, but Julia had remembered to bring her larger leather satchel, and the codex fit into it—just barely. They bid Julius farewell and walked on.

The narrow streets of the *subura* smelled pungent, the noise overwhelming, but Julia found both enjoyable anyway. She enjoyed watching the coppersmith, a small olive-skinned man from the eastern part of the empire, as he

---

[4]The word *parchment* comes from the name Pergamon. Parchment is animal skin, first produced in Pergamon.

sat on a little stool, banging away on a piece of copper to shape it into a pan. In the next shop down, a man sold spices, and the odors of frankincense, myrrh, cumin, dill, mint, cinnamon, and incense filled the air. Julia pictured the long journey these spices made as they travelled the spice road up from Arabia, past Petra, and onto the King's Highway beside Judaea, finally making their way west to the port of Caesarea Maritima and on to Roma.

Prisca's shop was currently making sandals, leather coverings for shields, extra-thick leggings for gladiators, and harnesses for the horses in the chariot races. The women watched as the workers scraped the skin so it could be cured by a smoking process. Another worker cut the leather into shapes, and a third waxed and then oiled it to provide a certain sheen.

Figure 18.3. Remnants of Roman sandals.

Julia loved to smell the leather once it had been properly waxed and oiled. The pleasant odor overcame her the minute she came into the small shop. The tanning process itself smelled horrible, so Prisca had moved that part of her operation to just outside the city gates across the Tiber.[5]

"Julia, in my teens there used to be a little cobbler's shop here, and he had a crow that could talk! He would greet the elites of the Forum in a formal and lavish way as they walked by. 'Salve,' he would say, 'new shoes for you, my prince,' and you know, it got that cobbler more business."[6]

---

[5]There were constant complaints from the social elites and even from ordinary workers about the noxious smells produced by all sorts of businesses in the *subura*. J. P. Morel, "The Craftsman," in *The Romans,* A. Giardina, ed. (University of Chicago Press, 1993), 217, chronicles the gradual shift of various industries out of the center of Rome to somewhere else. "The nauseating odors of the tannery works were relegated en masse *trans Tiberium.*"

[6]Pliny actually reports this anecdote as happening in the time of Tiberius. See Morel, "The Craftsman," 238.

Before Julia could remark on this astonishing tidbit, Prisca approached the man working on sandals. "You remember Valerius, don't you Julia?"

"Yes, indeed. He made the sandals I still wear today. He's the best at shaping leather."

"Which is why we've put him in charge of things here," Prisca said with a satisfied nod, Valerius beaming at the praise.

The two women walked into the back of the shop, where a large younger man with huge biceps was doing his best to stretch a piece of hide over the metal frame of a shield. He was using something like a wench to stretch and stretch and stretch some more.

Figure 18.4. A relief carving of a Roman gladiator.

"The trick here," said Justus in a deep, baritone voice, "is to stretch it just right so that no gaps or thin spots form in the leather."

"Goodness," said Julia with admiration, "you look the part of a gladiator yourself!"

"Well, that's because I was a gladiator, studying the art here in Roma, but then I fell in love with a young lady name Marcia who cared more about our future than my fame as a gladiator." He paused and cleared his throat, looking uncomfortable. His voice had been booming, but now he lowered it, barely audible above the noise of the shop. "And besides, I saw my best friend die in the arena. So, I figured it was time to give it up and have a family. They

offered me fifty-thousand gold aurei to continue, but I turned them down. It's a dangerous game, and nothing is worth more than my life and my wife, so here I am, making shields!"

Before leaving, Prisca sat down with Valerius to briefly go over the orders and the ledger. They had plenty of business right through to the end of the year, and so Prisca was satisfied. She approved the work, and said *"Vale,"* or "farewell," to all those in the shop, and she and Julia returned home. Prisca smiled all the way.

"Aquila would approve. We've done well since his passing," she said.

Julia linked her arm in Prisca's. It was rare for Prisca to speak of him unless it was in the stories she told of their past together, working for the cause of Christus. Julia was thankful that Prisca confided this fleeting thought to her, for it told her Prisca still thought of him during her days, missing his presence in them. "Yes. He certainly would," she quietly agreed.

19

HOUSE ARREST AND THE CAPTIVITY EPISTLES

Now I want you to know, brothers and sisters, that what has happened
to me has actually served to advance the gospel. As a result, it has
become clear throughout the whole palace guard and to everyone
else that I am in chains for Christ. And because of my chains, most
of the brothers and sisters have become confident in the Lord and
dare all the more to proclaim the gospel without fear. . . . Yes, and
I will continue to rejoice, for I know that through your prayers and
God's provision of the Spirit of Jesus Christ what has happened to me
will turn out for my deliverance. . . . All God's people here send you
greetings, especially those who belong to Caesar's household.

PHILIPPIANS 1:12-14, 18-19; 4:22

A Rome full of Greeks, yet few of the dregs are Greek!
For the Syrian Orontes has long since polluted the Tiber,
Bringing its language and customs, pipes and harp-strings,
And even their native timbrels are dragged along too,

And the girls forced to offer themselves in the Circus.

Go there, if your taste's a barbarous whore in a painted veil.

See, Romulus, those rustics of yours wearing Greek slippers,

Greek ointments, Greek prize medallions round their necks.

He's from the heights of Sicyon, and he's from Amydon,

From Andros, Samos, they come, from Tralles or Alabanda,

Seeking the Esquiline and the Viminal, named from its willows.

To become both the innards and masters of our great houses.

Quick witted, of shameless audacity, ready of speech, more

Lip than Isaeus, the rhetorician. Just say what you want them

To be. They'll bring you, in one person, whatever you need:

The teacher of languages, orator, painter, geometer, trainer,

Augur, rope-dancer, physician, magician, they know it all,

Your hungry Greeks: tell them to buzz off to heaven, they'll go.

That's why it was no Moroccan, Sarmatian, or man from Thrace

Who donned wings, but one Daedalus, born in the heart of Athens.

Should I not flee these people in purple? Should I watch them sign

Ahead of me, then, and recline to eat on a better couch than mine,

Men propelled to Rome by the wind, with the plums and the figs?

JUVENAL, SATIRE 3.61-62

JULIA UNDERSTOOD NOW why they hadn't continued yesterday afternoon, foregoing the story's progress for their pleasant visit into the *subura*. She could see when they resumed this morning that Prisca seemed agitated by what must be told.

"Now Julia, we've come to a place in the story just before the fire. I've told you many times about these events, so if you find me saying something amiss, please stop and correct me."

"Yes, Domina, but I doubt I shall need to do so. Your memory seems as sharp as ever."

Prisca sighed deeply and braced herself. "Back to the story then—"

"I'm trying to keep all the facts straight. Before we get started, would you tell me where Paulus had his house arrest?"

Prisca looked relieved at Julia's interruption, then surprised. "I've never told you that? It was in our home in the *subura* with Aquila and me, just like in former times in Corinth."[1]

Julia looked up with raised eyebrows. "Really? Tell me more."

Prisca was glad to think about that instead of what was to come. "They chained a centurion to him if he was on the move, and watched him at all times if he was at 'home.' Not surprisingly, since he had a captive audience, Paulus kept sharing the good news with these soldiers." Prisca chuckled. "Some of them groaned and said stop, some of them listened politely and laughed when he got to the part about the savior crucified by Roma, and some actually became followers of Jesus. Typical, indefatigable Paulus never ceased to share the good news."

"How did he use his time while he was in your home?"

"He met with both believers and synagogue leaders, as Luke relates at the end of his second chronicle. He also wrote to the Philippians and to the assembly in Colossae, which he'd not visited but which his coworker Tychicus had founded. And he wrote a circular document that cycled

---

[1] There has been a recent report of finding the house where Paulus was under house arrest, today buried beneath the Dora Pamphilj gallery in central Roma, between Via del Corso and Via della Gatta. See Matthew Cowden, "Paul's House Arrest Apartments Discovered?" www.matthew cowden.com/2016/10/23/pauls-house-arrest-apartments-discovered.

through Ephesus, Colossae, and other churches, and finally he wrote a personal appeal to Philemon. Would you like to hear more about this last remarkable letter?"[2]

"Absolutely! I've never read this letter, or even heard anything about it."

"Interesting. I may have entrusted that letter to the assembly." Prisca settled in, excited to share this story with her beloved daughter. "Philemon had worked with Paulus for some years. He hosted one of the assembly meetings in Colossae in his own home, and he had a slave named Onesimus, which was his nickname, as was the custom with most slaves. This name meant 'useful,' but 'useful' became 'useless' when he ran away from Colossae and eventually ended up here in Roma, where nearly half the population are slaves. Here a slave could easily disappear, but Onesimus sought Paulus, hoping he'd be an advocate with Philemon (Paulus had converted Philemon when he was in Asia some years before)."

"Why did Onesimus run away?"

"Ah, well. It appears he stole something from Philemon, but I never found out what, and when a fellow slave decided to turn him in, Onesimus panicked and fled. He might have gotten off with just a light beating, but Onesimus had a friend who was beaten to death by his owner, and he was scared of suffering a similar fate. It wasn't a rational fear, since Philemon was a good follower of Jesus who certainly taught and modeled nonviolence. Nevertheless, not four days after Paulus had arrived, Achilles went to our door, and there was a wet, bedraggled, bruised, smelly slave named Onesimus, asking for Paulus. He'd found us by asking other *Christianoi* he met in the *subura* where he might find the apostle to the Gentiles."

By now Julia was enchanted with this tale. "What did you do?"

---

[2]While some scholars have argued that Paul must have written these letters from Ephesus, there is no evidence Paul was ever under house arrest or incarcerated in Ephesus. See Ben Witherington, "The Case of the Imprisonment that Did Not Happen: Paul at Ephesus," *JETS* 60, no. 3 (2017), 525-32.

Prisca laughed at Julia's breathless response. "To his surprise, we took Onesimus in, and I put Clemens in charge of seeing he got cleaned up and had a dry tunic at least, before we let him see Paulus."

"Did Paulus know Onesimus?"

"He'd only seen him once, when he met Philemon, who was in Ephesus on business. Nevertheless, Paulus had a good pastoral side to his personality and lent a sympathetic ear to the slave's plight. In the process of several days, Paulus shared the good news that there were no slaves or free persons in Christus, and Onesimus quite readily swore his allegiance to 'the Lord Jesus Christus' thereafter. Paulus became fond of Onesimus, and even called him 'my spiritual child,' and Onesimus began to do tasks for Paulus."

"What kind of tasks?"

"Mostly little things. For instance, he often took messages to various other followers of Christus in Roma."

"So did he stay here in Roma? What happened to him?"

"Patience. I'm getting to that. The day came when Paulus was convinced Onesimus needed to go home and make amends with Philemon. So Paulus wrote a rather amazing personal letter to Philemon, gave it to Onesimus, sent him home, and promised he would try to come and make sure all was well in Colossae once his trial was over. Paulus concluded his letter to Philemon by saying, 'So if you consider me a partner, welcome him as you would welcome me. If he has done you any wrong or owes you anything, charge it to me. I, Paulus, am writing this with my own hand. I will pay it back—not to mention that you owe me your very self! I do wish, brother, that I may have some benefit from you in the Lord; refresh my heart in Christus. Confident of your obedience, I write to you, knowing that you will do even more than I ask.'"[3]

Julia looked up with a crooked smile. "Talk about arm-twisting persuasion!"

---

[3]Philemon 17-21.

"Yes." Prisca laughed. "Paulus even threatened to show up and stay in the guest room to make sure Philemon 'obeyed,' after earlier in the letter speaking of free and noncompulsory compliance. He also puns on Onesimus's name when he asks for 'benefit,' or 'use,' back from Philemon. Clearly, he wanted Philemon to return Onesimus as his coworker in Christus.

"But actually, the most important part of the letter is where Paulus says that Onesimus should not only be manumitted, he should be seen as no longer a slave but rather a brother in Christus."

"Is he saying what I think he's saying?"

Prisca nodded as comprehension dawned on Julia's face. "Paulus suggested that being in Christus means there should be no more slave or free, but instead brothers and sisters."

Julia was astounded. "This is a revolutionary idea in a world that depends on slaves for most manual or even skilled labor."

"It certainly is. To this day, genuine followers of Jesus have sought to buy slaves out of slavery, or to liberate those who had previously served as slaves in their homes or businesses. That's part of being a follower of Christus. After all, Paulus preached about the liberation of captives."

"So how did it all turn out for Onesimus?"

"He went on to become a Christian leader, an *episkopos,* or 'overseer,' in Ephesus—or so I've heard."

"What else happened when Paulus was under house arrest?"

"Perhaps most important were the four letters he wrote. We have copies of all four because, as you know, scribes make two copies of important documents. The first copies were left here, and the others sent to the assemblies in Asia and the Lycus Valley. These documents, especially the one called Ephesians, which is more of an oral sermon than a letter, Paulus chose to write in the rather verbose and colorful Asiatic rhetorical form, because those in that region found this style of rhetoric the most persuasive. Paulus knew how to be all things to all persons when it came to the art of persuasion.[4] As I said before, it was hard to say no to the man."

"I find the letters interesting. Tell me more about them."

"They are each fascinating letters. Take the one to the Philippians. Two things surprise me as I read it now. One, he clearly expected to be delivered from house arrest, and two, he dearly loves the Philippians. They certainly loved him too, regularly sending him financial support."

"I remember Paulus mentioning Euodia and Syntyche in that letter. Who were they?"

"They were two female leaders in that assembly. Paulus had no issues with women leaders in his congregations. Euodia is in fact the same person Luke calls 'the Lydian,' who was the first convert in that town."[5]

Prisca pondered a moment. "There is so much more I could say about these four letters, but we must turn to Paulus's appearance before Nero. That deserves a whole day's chronicling . . . tomorrow."

---

[4] Epideictic rhetoric is the rhetoric of praise and blame. Rather than involving arguments, it lifts up key qualities, virtues to emulate, or vices to avoid. See Ben Witherington, *New Testament Rhetoric* (Eugene, OR: Wipf and Stock, 2009).

[5] Acts 16 and Philippians 4. Lydia may be a personal name in Acts 16, but it may be a description—the person from Lydia, and so, the Lydian.

20

THE RELEASE OF THE APOSTLE

By reason of jealousy and strife Paulus by his example pointed out the prize of patient endurance. After that he had been seven times in bonds, had been driven into exile, had been stoned, had preached in the East and in the West, he won the noble renown which was the reward of his faith, having taught righteousness unto the whole world and having reached the farthest bounds of the West; and when he had borne his testimony before the rulers, so he departed from the world and went unto the holy place, having been found a notable pattern of patient endurance.

1 CLEMENT 5.5-6

They declared that the sum total of their guilt or error amounted to no more than this; they had met regularly before dawn on a fixed day to chant verses alternately among themselves in honor of Christ as if

---

Quotation from Pliny the Younger: The fair-minded Romans had a hard time finding much wrong with Christian practice, other than it was a "*superstitio.*" See the discussion in R. L. Wilken, *The Christians as the Romans Saw Them* (New Haven: Yale University Press, 1984), 1-30. Pliny is the earliest Roman official to comment at some length about Christians in the early second century AD.

of a god, and also to bind themselves by oath, not for any criminal purpose, but to abstain from theft, robbery, and adultery, and to commit no breach of trust and not to deny a deposit when called upon to restore it. After this ceremony it had been their custom to disperse and reassemble later to take food of an ordinary, harmless kind.

PLINY THE YOUNGER, *EPISTLE 96*

AS JULIA DRESSED FOR THE DAY, her thoughts roamed over what she knew was coming next in Prisca's story. *I must be encouraging and patient, as this part of the story will be difficult for her, but it needs to be made clear. Many Christus followers are in the dark about what happened with Paulus, and with the Christianoi in Roma just before and after the fire.*

Prisca, for her part, had summoned her courage and looked forward to getting through and beyond this part of her tale. They sat once more at the *tablinum* to make it easier for Julia to write, and so Prisca could speak in a normal tone of voice. She jumped right in without hesitation.

"As I said before, Roman law favors Roman citizens. But there is another factor as well. If someone makes a serious accusation against a Roman citizen, that person needs to appear in court *in person*. Paulus, who had appealed to Caesar himself, waited and waited, but no one from Jerusalem showed up to make an accusation against him. No one. Indeed, they hadn't even bothered to communicate with Jewish authorities in Roma. This is how Luke tells what happened when Paulus met with the local Jewish authorities."[1] Prisca handed Julia the document to copy.

---

[1] About the development of Roman law in the first century, and the increasing role of the emperor in capital cases, see Olivia F. Robinson, *The Criminal Law of Ancient Rome* (Baltimore: Johns Hopkins University Press, 1995).

Three days later he called together the local Jewish leaders. When they had assembled, Paulus said to them: "My brothers, although I have done nothing against our people or against the customs of our ancestors, I was arrested in Jerusalem and handed over to the Romans. They examined me and wanted to release me, because I was not guilty of any crime deserving death. The Jews objected, so I was compelled to make an appeal to Caesar. I certainly did not intend to bring any charge against my own people. For this reason, I have asked to see you and talk with you. It is because of the hope of Israel that I am bound with this chain."[2]

They replied, "We have not received any letters from Judea concerning you, and none of our people who have come from there has reported or said anything bad about you. But we want to hear what your views are, for we know that people everywhere are talking against this sect."

They arranged to meet Paulus on a certain day, and came in even larger numbers to the place where he was staying. He witnessed to them from morning till evening, explaining about the kingdom of God, and from the Law of Moses and from the Prophets he tried to persuade them about Jesus. Some were convinced by what he said, but others would not believe.[3]

"As usual, Paulus turned adversity into an opportunity." Prisca popped a morsel in her mouth, chewing slowly. After swallowing, she went on.

"The outcome was actually rather predictable under these circumstances, especially since Seneca and Burrus were still running things. Paulus was taken to the court in the Forum one morning, after having been here for two years, but the emperor didn't bother to show up. Instead, a clerk handed

---

[2]On the development of the whole theology of the noble death by martyrdom, see G. W. Bowersock, *Martyrdom and Rome* (Cambridge: Cambridge University Press, 1995).
[3]Acts 28:17-25.

Paulus a letter dismissing the trial because of lack of evidence, and because the proconsul in Judaea said there was no basis for a guilty verdict. It was a great day, and the communities of Christus in Roma celebrated this victory."[4]

"So, did Paulus stay in Roma after that?"

Prisca shook her head. "Typically, Paulus didn't celebrate long or rest on his past laurels. He felt he needed to get back east and check on several troublesome congregations, but first he would make an initial trip to Spain, with the traveling money the Roman Christus followers had raised for him to do so. This took a good year of his life and didn't accomplish much other than an initial survey of a mission field. Paulus continued to be hampered by his physical affliction, and Luke, his usual traveling companion of late, decided to stay in Roma and finish writing his own chronicle of the earliest days of our movement."

"Why do you think Luke made that decision?"

"He wanted to explain how the Good News had arrived in the Eternal City and was successfully being shared here. He didn't want to turn his volume into a biography of the rise and fall of Paulus—or Peter for that matter, who still had not arrived in Roma."

"Domina, when did Peter arrive in Roma?"

"It was shortly after Paulus left for Spain. They were rather like ships passing in the night. But let's save that story for this afternoon."

Achilles brought the two women their usual midday meal—broth, fruit, nuts, some bread and dipping sauce, and a little wine. They ate, mostly lost

---

[4]The vicious accusations against Christians do not begin before the mid- to late-second century AD, when we begin to hear of suspicions not only of gross immorality but of cannibalism (based apparently on the Lord's Supper words *this is my body*) and of practicing secret and even magic rites. The most virulent of the haters of Christianity in the second century seems to have been Marcus Cornelius Fronto, a rhetorician and teacher of two future emperors, Marcus Aurelius and Lucius Verus. We know of his kind of arguments through a Christian document written by Minucius Felix written around AD 200, presenting a dialogue between a pagan and a Christian, with Felix serving as moderator. See the discussion in Stephen Benko, *Pagan Rome and the Early Christians* (Bloomington, IN: Indiana University Press, 1984), 54-78.

in their own thoughts, Julia preoccupied with when the centurion should be arriving in the next day or so to take Prisca to the tribunal. "I must redouble my prayers," she murmured to herself.

"What?" Prisca asked as she reclined on the couch opposite Julia in the *triclinium*.

"Oh nothing, Domina. Nothing."

After the midday meal, they returned to the *tablinum*.

"So, about Peter's arrival in Roma."

"Yes, it was not a week after Paulus left for Spain that Peter arrived. He'd been to many places in Asia and north and west of Asia, but had finally made it to what he was to call 'Babylon.' Because he was 'the apostle to the circumcised,' he met first with the Jewish followers of Jesus here, and then with the Gentiles. The Gentiles were not thrilled with this order of visitation, since Peter was the chief apostle of the church in Jerusalem and the leader of the Twelve during Jesus' ministry."

"What did you think of that, Domina?"

Prisca's look became determined. "As I argued then, it was only right that Peter do it this way, because as Paulus himself said in his letter to us, the good news is for the Jew first."

Julia nodded, satisfied with her answer.

"The main thing he wanted us to know is that many Jews were coming to Christus in all sorts of places, and this was a report we'd not heard before. In fact, we hadn't heard anything about Peter for several years, until he showed up here. As it turns out, he'd been concentrating on Jews in some of the areas and cities that were less well known in the empire. He spoke of God's elect, exiles scattered throughout the provinces of Pontus, Galatia, Cappadocia, Asia, and Bithynia."

"How did they become exiles in all those places?"

"The Roman army enslaved and then moved many Jews to these provinces for the purpose of serving as workers, educators, and administrators of various sorts. What Peter found was that many of them had become so Hellenized that they were virtually indistinguishable from the Gentiles. They went to the games, some even participated in the games, having their circumcision undone or disguised. They dressed like Gentiles, sometimes ate with Gentiles, shopped with Gentiles. They had blended into their Gentile-dominant environment to such a degree that they hardly seemed like Jews at all, and Peter had to address that."

Julia nodded. "How did the church in Roma respond to Peter?"

"Here, followers of Christus greatly respected Peter, and he respected them enough to not assert his authority or take over and manage all the assemblies, even of the Jewish believers. Instead, he told his stories and rehearsed some interesting anecdotes from the life of Jesus.

"John Mark also showed up during this period, and became Peter's assistant, translating Peter's earlier Aramaic reflections on the life of Jesus into serviceable Greek."[5]

"Anyone else?"

Prisca thought a moment. "Silas was also with Peter and planned to help him compose a letter to Peter's assemblies." Prisca fell silent and her face reflected pain. "All seemed calm. None of us could have imagined the disaster that came next." She stood up and smoothed her robe, throwing off her gloomy thoughts. "That tale must surely wait until tomorrow. I need to muster my courage tonight, and say a few prayers before I tell that story."

Julia worried. Prisca had put off her tale once more. She was afraid the telling of it would be too much for her mother to endure, along with her other trial to come.

---

[5]This is what Papias tells us. Peter's memoirs of Jesus and his teaching are said to have become Mark's Gospel. The title of Papias's work is *Oracles of the Lord,* and today it is mostly culled from Eusebius' later *Ecclesiastical History.* See Peter Kirby, "Fragments of Papias," Early Christian Writings, www.earlychristianwritings.com/text/papias.html.

21

THE CONFLAGRATION

Seneca to Paul: "The source of the many fires which Rome suffers is plain. But if humble men could speak out what the reason is, and if it were possible to speak without risk in this dark time, all would be plain to all. Christians and Jews are commonly executed as contrivers of the fire. Whoever the criminal is whose pleasure is that of a butcher, and who veils himself with a lie, he is reserved for his due season: and as the best of men is sacrificed, the one for the many, so he, vowed to death for all, will be burned with fire. A hundred and thirty-two houses and four blocks have been burnt in six days, the seventh brought a pause."

THE [APOCRYPHAL] CORRESPONDENCE
OF PAUL AND SENECA 12

HOWEVER, THE NEXT DAY, resourceful Prisca surprised Julia once again. "As you know, dear Julia, I've had a hard time talking about this, because of what happened to us. So, yesterday I asked Clemens to visit Tacitus, who is currently in the process of writing a chronicle of Roman

---

Quotation from The [Apocryphal] Correspondence: This document dates probably to the third century AD and is fictional, but it shows how the impact of the fire on the fledgling Christian community was so severe, they were still talking about it and explaining it centuries later.

history of the relevant period. It's not available yet to all of Roma, but I have a friend who works in his household who got permission to copy out an excerpt. Would you copy it into our record? I believe that will save me the pain of rehearsing it once again."

"Of course! What a good idea." Julia took the document and began to copy.

Now started the most terrible and destructive fire which Roma had ever experienced. It began in the Circus, where it adjoins the Palatine and Caelian hills. Breaking out in shops selling flammable goods, and fanned by the wind, the conflagration instantly grew and swept the whole length of the Circus. There were no walled mansions or temples, or any other obstructions, which could arrest it. First, the fire swept violently over the level spaces. Then it climbed the hills—but returned to ravage the lower ground again. It outstripped every counter-measure. The ancient city's narrow winding streets and irregular blocks encouraged its progress.

Terrified, shrieking women, helpless old and young, people intent on their own safety, people unselfishly supporting invalids or waiting for them, fugitives and lingerers alike—all heightened the confusion. When people looked back, menacing flames sprang up before them or outflanked them. When they escaped to a neighboring quarter, the fire followed—even districts believed remote proved to be involved. Finally, with no idea where or what to flee, they crowded onto the country roads, or lay in the fields. Some who had lost everything—even their food for the day—could have escaped, but preferred to die. So did others, who had failed to rescue their loved ones. Nobody dared fight the flames. Attempts to do so were prevented by menacing gangs. Torches, too, were openly thrown in, by men crying that they acted under orders. Perhaps they had received orders. Or they may just have wanted to plunder unhampered.[1]

---

[1] Tacitus, *Annals* 15.

When she finished, she looked up at Prisca. "Would you like to say anything else about your experience, or is it too difficult?"

Prisca stood to look outside. After a few moments of silence, she said, "I confess, I was one of those shrieking, terrified women, because the shop right next to where we worked caught fire, and, not surprisingly, I panicked. Aquila kept trying to calm me, with no success. Suddenly, he came up with an inspiration. He would run to our shop after packing some supplies from the house, grab a tent, and we would flee—out of town and into the fields. It took us about an hour to get these two things accomplished, and by this time our apartment was well and truly in flames. Most of the *subura* was, because it's where the fire started. And I can tell you right now—it was set! As Tacitus says, there were gangs standing around preventing the *vigiles urbani* from helping. I saw one gang member with a torch in his hand. When we first saw the fire burning, I remembered what my teacher had taught me

Figure 21.1. The fire of Rome.

as a girl about the nature of the world according to the Stoics; namely, this world consists of a fire or a spirit that animates everything, and eventually our world will burn out in a final great conflagration, after which, like a phoenix, it will rise from the ashes and begin again. I decided not to wait to see if this would come true. I panicked and we ran for our lives.

"We first went up the Palatine hill, and that's when we heard Nero playing his lyre while watching the fire—disgusting! Nero was only sixteen when he became emperor, and we expected there would be some youthful errors and excess, but when the fire broke out Nero was twenty-six, and there could

Figure 21.2. Nero and the burning of Rome.

be no excuse for him not merely watching it burn but probably having the fire lit in the first place so he could fulfill his egocentric dreams of rebuilding a goodly part of Roma according to his own designs.

"We headed to the gate beyond that hill, and I made the mistake of turning around like Lot's wife, and I saw the flames roaring up the hill. This was to be the stuff of my nightmares. I see it again and again. And the smells, Julia—the smells! Not just wood or leather burning, but human flesh! It was indescribably awful. And then it happened. I doubt you even remember it. There was a tiny girl, screaming, soot on her face, wearing what I can only describe as a grain sack. Julia . . ."

And then Julia dropped her stylus and moved to embrace Prisca so her mother wouldn't have to say any more. They both clung to each other, and when Julia felt her mother's body begin to quietly heave, she felt herself give way to sobbing too, as if both of them had bottled up thirty years of emotion.

Neither felt the need to speak for a long time, but when she was ready, Prisca managed to find her voice again.

"Despite all the horrors of the fire, despite the loss of our home, despite the damage to our workplace, God placed you in our path, so we would rescue you. Something wonderful was to come out of that disaster. I finally had a daughter, though of course I didn't know that at the time. I was in too much shock, but Aquila had the good sense to say, 'Come! We must take her with us, and find out later if she's just lost.'"

Prisca was still embracing Julia as she told this part of her daugher's story, but now she pulled back to look at her. "You were barely two. I guess we will never know exactly. You were too young to tell us if you had parents. By the look of you, you'd been scrounging for food and a place to sleep on the streets. You seemed to us one of the many starving children of Roma. There were hundreds of them at that time.

"And so we wandered together to a pasture just north of the city gate, where we pitched our tent and watched the horrible procession of people fleeing the city by any means possible: ox carts, on horses, some wealthy persons being carried in *lectica* with curtains shielding them from our view, carried by enormous, muscular slaves.[2] People were running in bare feet, shouting, cursing, crying... unbelievable! It was about this moment, while you and I were sitting together in the mouth of the tent, that you leaned against me. I gave you a hug, and the next thing I knew, you were sound asleep on my lap. And I don't know how to explain what came over me, but I knew in that moment, I'd care for you with my dying breath."

---

[2] A *lectica* is a litter. According to archaeologists and scientists, the average height of a Roman man was 5'4" while a woman was 5'1", with weights on average of 143 and 108 pounds, respectively. Slaves from Gaul or Africa could be much taller than this and were able to see over the crowds of Romans when they bore a litter through the streets. See Angelo Angela, *A Day in the Life of Ancient Rome* (New York: Europa Editions, 2009), 172.

22

PETER TAKES CHARGE AND WRITES OF SUFFERING

As soon as I send Artemas or Tychicus to you, do your best to come to me at Nicopolis, because I have decided to winter there. Do everything you can to help Zenas the lawyer and Apollos on their way and see that they have everything they need. Our people must learn to devote themselves to doing what is good, in order to provide for urgent needs and not live unproductive lives.

TITUS 3:12-14

EMOTIONALLY SPENT AS THEY WERE, mother and daughter couldn't face continuing their tale that day. Instead, they laughed, cried again, and took the rest of the day to celebrate all that God had given them together. It was tremendously healing to Prisca, and Julia felt anew God's guiding hand on their lives. A day she'd worried would be painful ended up being of great comfort—so much so that Prisca was able to pick up the tale once again the next morning.

"Peter took charge at that point," she began. "He guided the Christus followers, both Jew and Gentile, to the catacombs as a place of refuge. As it turned out, this was farsighted. He couldn't have known *Christianoi* would be blamed for the fire, but he intuited that it couldn't mean anything good for those of our faith. After all, Paulus was out of town, and Andronicus and Junia had gone with him. Peter was the only apostle we had."

"Where in the catacombs did we go?"

Prisca sat up a little straighter. "To my family's, the so-called catacombs of Priscilla on the Via Salaria. A painting of my stepmother, Priscilla, on the wall comforted me when we went there." Prisca added in a quiet voice, "Maybe I can take you there now so you can see it for yourself. I haven't been able to face it since we left."

Both women fell quiet until Prisca felt ready to continue. "Originally the followers of Jesus went to the sand quarry area called the *arenarium*, but as the cry against us all grew, we went further underground into the *cryptoporticus* and finally to the *hypogaeum*.

Figure 22.1. Agape feast painted in a catacomb.

"We would do everything underground during this period, including sharing meals.

"But, of course, our surroundings constantly reminded us that we were among the dead.

"I wrote Paulus and sent a letter via a Christus follower going to Tarraco, Spain, where we thought Paulus was, but it didn't reach him. Paulus didn't return to Roma for more than a year, and when he came he was in chains, thrown into the Mamertinus. But I am getting ahead of myself. Back to Peter . . .

"As we began to meet in the catacombs, Peter wrote a lengthy letter about suffering as Christus had suffered. He explained that Christus fulfilled the role of suffering servant that Isaiah spoke of many centuries prior. Peter asked Silas—or to use his Roman name, Silvanus—to read this letter to us before sending it to its multiple destinations in Asia and elsewhere.[1] Julia, let's put a bit of it into our chronicle because it gives a good sense of how we were thinking about things then, dreading the coming persecution as vicious rumors spread."

Julia left and eventually came back with a dog-eared scroll in hand. "It took some time, Domina. I thought I knew where it was, but I was wrong and had to ask Clemens."

Prisca unrolled the scroll, and then pointed to a particular line. "Start reading here, and I'll let you know when to stop."

In all this you greatly rejoice, though now for a little while you may have had to suffer grief in all kinds of trials. These have come so that the proven genuineness of your faith—of greater worth than gold, which perishes even though refined by fire—may result in praise, glory and honor when Jesus Christus is revealed. Though you have not seen him, you love him; and even though you do not see him now, you believe in him and are filled with an inexpressible and glorious joy, for you are receiving the end result of your faith, the salvation of your souls.[2]

---

[1]See 1 Peter 5.12-13 on Silvanus, and also Mark.
[2]1 Peter 1:6-9.

"All right, stop right there, and read again, from here."

> Live such good lives among the pagans that, though they accuse you
> of doing wrong, they may see your good deeds and glorify God on
> the day he visits us.
>
> Submit yourselves for the Lord's sake to every human au-
> thority: whether to the emperor, as the supreme authority, or to gov-
> ernors, who are sent by him to punish those who do wrong and to
> commend those who do right. For it is God's will that by doing good
> you should silence the ignorant talk of foolish people. Live as free
> people, but do not use your freedom as a cover-up for evil; live as
> God's slaves. Show proper respect to everyone, love the family of
> believers, fear God, honor the emperor.[3]

"And then finally read this, from a little further in the speech."

> To this you were called, because Christus suffered for you, leaving you
> an example, that you should follow in his steps.
>> He committed no sin,
>> and no deceit was found in his mouth.
> When they hurled their insults at him, he did not retaliate; when
> he suffered, he made no threats. Instead, he entrusted himself to him
> who judges justly. 'He himself bore our sins' in his body on the cross, so
> that we might die to sins and live for righteousness; "by his wounds
> you have been healed." For "you were like sheep going astray," but now
> you have returned to the Shepherd and Overseer of your souls.[4]

Prisca said, "You can see what he was doing. On the one hand, he reminded them to be respectful of the governing authorities, even if they are
abusive. He preached the ethic of nonviolence—or put positively, the ethic

---

[3] 1 Peter 2:13-17.
[4] 1 Peter 2:21-25.

of love—even toward one's tormentors, the ethic that Jesus himself preached. He envisioned the possibility not only of a persecution here in Roma but elsewhere in the empire as well, and he wanted one and all to respond not with anger and hatred but with nonviolence and love. And as it turns out, he was right. There would be more persecutions, and various martyrs as well."

Julia was suddenly curious. "What was the difference between Peter and Paulus in the way they worked with people?"

"People have overblown the differences and tried to pit Peter against Paulus, or Jacob against Paulus, but this is largely wrong. Neither Peter nor Jacob agreed with the Judaizers among the Christus followers, those who wanted Gentile converts to fully convert to Judaism. Jacob, however, remained true to Torah, being in Jerusalem, and trying to win over Jews to Jesus, and Peter's praxis varied, depending on whether he was with Jews or Gentiles."[5] Prisca paused and looked into the distance. "I respected that about him."

Then she focused back to the task at hand. "Paulus saw more clearly where things were going if many Gentiles became followers of Jesus. Among other things, it meant Jews would need to forego some of the strictures about food laws and the like. For those of us who had only progressed as far as being a God fearer in the synagogue, this was not much of an issue. Yes, there were arguments in the Jerusalem assembly about proper praxis, but even those arguments were largely settled at the Jerusalem council just after Paulus's first missionary journey. To my knowledge, there were not any memorable *theological* arguments about what we should believe about Christus, the cross, or the resurrection, but clearly it was Paulus—and to a lesser degree, Peter—who saw the theological implications of our faith. And one implication was, sadly, that with the growth in Gentile converts, Jews

---

[5] I take it that Galatians 2 makes clear Peter was prepared to eat with Gentiles even at a Gentile house, and so it seems to imply he was prepared to eat non-kosher food. See also Acts 10.

were less and less likely to join a Gentile-majority religious group. As of now, at least in Roma, Jewish followers of Jesus, who were always a minority, are now an even *smaller* minority, and I fear the future will not be bright for Jewish followers of Jesus."

Prisca once again fell silent, dreading what must follow. "Shortly I must tell you about Apollos's sermon written to Jewish believers here in Roma, but first we need to talk about Nero's actual persecutions."

"Wait, Domina. There is something further I don't quite understand. Was there some sort of personal tension between Peter and Paulus? Did they not get along well as brothers in Christus? Did they avoid each other at times?"

"Why do you ask?"

"Well, I remember you telling the story of Paulus and Peter in Antioch, before Paulus wrote the first letter to the Galatians. Paulus confronted Peter in public, presumably in the assembly meeting, about his hypocrisy of first dining with Gentiles, and then backing off under pressure from the men who came from Jacob in Jerusalem. Did Peter agree with him?"

Prisca nodded confidently. "Paulus talked to us about that confrontation in Antioch when we were with him in Corinth. Paulus had a temper and was not shy about expressing his feelings. He later regretted blowing up at Peter in front of others. They should have talked privately. That incident created a certain tension between the two men. I don't know if it was ever entirely healed. They respected each other and particularly each other's work, but they mostly stayed out of each other's way, even when working in the same area. Peter focused mainly on Jews, Paulus on Gentiles. But Peter defended Paulus's proclamation of salvation by grace through faith in Jesus at the Jerusalem Council in the middle of this century.[6] That marginalized the Judaizing position, especially since Jacob officially ruled that Gentiles simply needed to stay out of the pagan temples where idolatry and

---

[6]Acts 15.

immorality are rife. That whole series of events not only helped validate Paulus's mission, but it created a bit more respect and rapport between Paulus and Peter. They never actually worked together hand in hand, but like persons acting in the same drama, they both played important roles and have helped make the assembly of God what it is today."

"That helps me understand a bit better, but it seems sad they never fully reconciled."

Prisca looked weighed down by what her daughter had said. "Julia, we are all imperfect people, and yet those are the only kinds of people God has to work with, and by his grace and love he has chosen to do so. So, we must not judge those men too harshly. They were never rivals. They both worked for the same cause, the same King, the same kingdom. But they were very different persons with very different personalities. Peter may have envied Paulus's success in winning Gentiles; Paulus may have envied Peter's personal knowledge of and relationship with Jesus. But neither man said so because they knew what really mattered was that they served the same risen Lord. That outweighed everything. As Paulus used to say, 'We must not dwell on the past, but we must learn from it,' and I think both men did that."

Julia absorbed the wisdom of these words, but she couldn't ponder them long, since Prisca went bravely on, her jaw set and her eyes narrowed. "But now we must turn to another tragic part of the story."

23

CHRISTUS FOLLOWERS AS ROMAN CANDLES

Accordingly, an arrest was first made of all who pleaded guilty; then, upon their information, an immense multitude was convicted, not so much of the crime of firing the city, as of hatred against mankind. Mockery of every sort was added to their deaths. Covered with the skins of beasts, they were torn by dogs and perished, or were nailed to crosses, or were doomed to the flames and burnt, to serve as a nightly illumination, when daylight had expired. Nero offered his gardens for the spectacle, and was exhibiting a show in the circus, while he mingled with the people in the dress of a charioteer or stood aloft on a car. Hence, even for criminals who deserved extreme and exemplary punishment, there arose a feeling of compassion; for it was not, as it seemed, for the public good, but to satiate one man's cruelty, that they were being destroyed.

TACITUS, *ANNALS*, 15.44

SOMEHOW PRISCA MANAGED TO WORK HER WAY through the worst part of the story without more trauma or nightmares. But there was still a good deal to address. It was a chilly morning, so she and Julia decided to retreat into the enclosed bedroom next to the brazier. They each drank a hot beverage, and Julia blew on her hands before taking dictation.

"Domina, how exactly did Christus followers who were hiding in the catacombs hear about Nero's torments, and how did Nero's soldiers find them? I'm too young to remember."

But just as Prisca was about to speak, a breathless Achilles ran into the room. "Domina, there is a centurion at the door."

Julia felt like someone had put tongs on her heart, and she became as breathless as Achilles. Prisca paled, but then looked resolute. Slowly gathering herself, she made her way to the front entrance.

Figure 23.1. Christians were mauled by beasts in the *circus maximus*.

"Yes?" she queried the tall man in full regalia.

In a strong and authoritarian voice he said, "Be ready in the morning, as I will come to take you to the tribunal. Hail, Domitianus!" And then he pounded his chest with one fist and departed.

Visibly shaken, Prisca returned to her room and to the brazier, and Julia could see she was shivering, but not primarily from the cold. Julia moved

next to her and took her in her arms. "Don't worry, Domina. We are all in the Lord's hands." She winced a little as the words came out of her mouth. Her mother knew this better than anyone, and she despised that she made such a fearful thing sound trite.

But Prisca hugged her back. "A timely reminder. Sometimes I feel abandoned and need to be reminded so."

They both stared into the fire for a few moments, but then Prisca took Julia's hands. "Would you pray for me right now?"

"Of course!" Julia got down on her knees in front of Prisca. "Dear Lord, this is the only mother I have known. Please don't take her away from me now. We have journeyed far in faith together since we lost Aquila, and we would be grateful to finish on a more joyful note. We know you can work all things together for good for those who love you, and we do love you with our whole hearts, so we lay our petition before you, in your Son's precious name. Amen."

"Amen," Prisca added. "I could not have put it better."

"Would you like to take the rest of the day off, Domina?"

Prisca shook her head vigorously. "Absolutely not! It's all the more vital to finish our tale."

Julia let go of Prisca's hands and reluctantly picked up her stylus, amazed at this woman's courage. Before she could position herself to write, Prisca began again. "It probably doesn't need a lot of gruesome elaboration, but there were dozens of *Christianoi* who lost their lives either being set alight or being mauled by beasts."

"Oh, Domina!" Julia cried, horrified by the thought. "How can you talk about this right now?"

Prisca laid a comforting hand on Julia's arm. "There is a story, which may be just a legend, that when some of our fellow believers were set on fire, they began singing a hymn to Christus. This maddened Nero. He kept asking 'Why are they singing? How could they possibly be singing?' He could not understand that greater is he who is within them, producing their joy and power to overcome trials, than any force in this world. That is how I can talk about it."

Julia felt humbled but still couldn't find the courage Prisca had. She wrote furiously because it kept her thoughts from running wild.

"There were dozens and dozens of burials during that sad time, and the community of Jewish believers diminished even further." Her next words came in a rush. "Unexpectedly, they apprehended my Aquila in the market and, without my even knowing, took him to the circus, where he was mauled by a lion." Her rush of words stopped abruptly, and Julia could barely hear as she muttered, "He died shortly thereafter."

Julia couldn't write the words when she looked up and saw the tears flowing down Prisca's cheeks. Her own throat was so tight she couldn't even force any words of comfort past her lips, but somehow Prisca choked out another sentence. "Oh, Julia, I don't know what I would have done if I hadn't had you."

Julia tried to control her tears. She wanted to be strong for Prisca's sake, but in her effort, her sobs came out in strange barks of grief.

Prisca looked at her daughter with compassion, knowing Julia might soon know the kind of loss Prisca had endured. Finally, she found her voice. "I'm sorry, Julia. Life is fragile, very fragile, and can disappear in a moment. I wish I could spare you such grief."

There was silence, as unhappiness reigned.

24

BURNED OUT
CHRISTIANOI—
THE TEMPTATION
TO DEFECT

Why do you act the part of a Jew, when you are a Greek? Do you not see how each is called a Jew, or a Syrian or an Egyptian? and when we see a man inclining to two sides, we are accustomed to say: "This man is not a Jew, but he acts as one." But when he has assumed the affectations of one who has been imbued with Jewish doctrine and has adopted that sect, then he is in fact and he is named a Jew. Thus we too being falsely imbued (baptized), are in name Jews, but in fact we are something else. Our feelings are inconsistent with our words; we are far from practicing what we say, and that of which we are proud, as if we knew it.

EPICTETUS, *DISCOURSES* 2.9

WHEN BOTH WOMEN HAD RECOVERED, Prisca looked tenacious. Somehow the pressure of the next day gave her courage and kept her on task to finish her story before the tribunal interrupted. "Julia, I know this is difficult, but we must keep going. I haven't covered Apollos's response to this situation yet, or the death of Peter and Paulus. We must keep writing this evening. Can you find the strength?"

Julia nodded, wiping her tears with a handkerchief she kept tucked in her sleeve. She'd barely picked up her stylus when Prisca began again.

"Most horrifying, we were betrayed by our fellow believers who committed apostasy under duress and told the authorities where to find us. We survived because they almost exclusively arrested men, especially Jewish men.

"There was a great temptation to abandon Christus. Apollos gave a powerful sermon to help us. He reflected Paulus's teaching, but the sermon was uniquely his own. He focused on Christus as our heavenly high priest and created a marvelous image of a sanctuary that is both on earth and in heaven, with the holy of holies being in heaven, and Christus serving as both priest and sacrifice, offering himself, and then applying the blood in the holy of holies to truly atone for all our sins. He made clear that Christus's death was a once-for-all-time, once-for-all-persons sacrifice, making obsolete the sacrificial system of the Mosaic law.

"He did an even better job than Paulus, if I may say so, of making clear that the new covenant is indeed a *new* covenant, not merely a renewal of the Mosaic one. This was a vital point to Jewish followers of Jesus that were contemplating hiding within Judaism and renouncing Christus. At one point in his beautiful epideictic sermon, in praise of faith, Apollos sternly warned that to give up one's faith in Christus is apostasy; it is crucifying Christus afresh. It's not a return to normalcy in Judaism; it is apostasy, even for a Jew. I've already found the scroll. Please copy from here:"

> We must pay the most careful attention, therefore, to what we have heard, so that we do not drift away. For since the message spoken through angels was binding, and every violation and disobedience received its just punishment, how shall we escape if we ignore

so great a salvation? This salvation, which was first announced by the Lord, was confirmed to us by those who heard him. God also testified to it by signs, wonders and various miracles, and by gifts of the Holy Spirit distributed according to his will.[1]

"And then let us add the following:"

See to it, brothers and sisters, that none of you has a sinful, unbelieving heart that turns away from the living God. But encourage one another daily, as long as it is called "Today," so that none of you may be hardened by sin's deceitfulness. We have come to share in Christus, if indeed we hold our original conviction firmly to the very end. As has just been said:

"Today, if you hear his voice,
  do not harden your hearts
  as you did in the rebellion."[2]

"One more selection will help:"

Therefore, let us move beyond the elementary teachings about Christ and be taken forward to maturity, not laying again the foundation of repentance from acts that lead to death, and of faith in God, instruction about cleansing rites, the laying on of hands, the resurrection of the dead, and eternal judgment. And, God permitting, we will do so.

It is impossible for those who have once been enlightened, who have tasted the heavenly gift, who have shared in the Holy Spirit, who have tasted the goodness of the word of God and the powers of the coming age and who have fallen away, to be brought back to repentance. To their loss they are crucifying the Son of God all over again and subjecting him to public disgrace. Land that drinks in the rain

---

[1] Hebrews 2:1-4.
[2] Hebrews 3:12-15.

often falling on it and that produces a crop useful to those for whom it is farmed receives the blessing of God. But land that produces thorns and thistles is worthless and is in danger of being cursed. In the end, it will be burned.

Even though we speak like this, dear friends, we are convinced of better things in your case—the things that have to do with salvation.[3]

"As you can see, the warnings became more and more severe as the discourse progressed, and some of this rhetoric is no doubt hyperbolic, to try and prevent the audience from defecting. But Apollos does not leave the audience on a negative note; there's also that wonderful description, which I call the 'hall of faith,' where we learn that faith is forward looking, not dwelling in the past—it is 'the confidence of what we hope for and assurance about what we do not see.'"[4]

Prisca had been speaking rapidly, spilling out a great torrent of words, but now she slowed down and Julia could see the pain mingled with joy on her face. "It was precisely this that I clung to when I lost my Aquila, my rock. I also loved the image of us following Christus into eternity, with him as the prime example of true faith and faithfulness, him as the trailblazer and finisher of faith. Apollos's pleas did not entirely fall on deaf ears, but then just when we thought things couldn't get worse, we lost Peter and then Paulus."

Julia wrote furiously trying to keep up. When she finished writing, Prisca said, "It would be wise for me to relate first of Paulus's journey back east . . ." She then choked on her next words. "If I'm still here tomorrow."

As she noticed tears welling in Julia's eyes again, she quickly added, "Let's not grieve yet. We'll see what tomorrow brings. The Lord didn't promise escape from suffering, but he promised to be with us through it all. And that's a very great comfort."

---

[3]Hebrews 6:1-9.
[4]Hebrews 11:1.

25

A SURPRISE ENDING, AND A RETURN TO THE EAST

ON THE MORNING OF SEPTEMBER 18, Prisca steeled herself to face the ordeal of the tribunal before Domitianus, but the centurion never came.[1]

About lunchtime, Achilles answered a knock on the door. A neighbor stood there looking anxious yet clearly relieved. "Have you heard the latest news?"

"No, what news?"

"Domitianus was assassinated by his court officials, and Nerva, his one-time advisor, is now in charge."

Achilles looked thunderstruck. "What? Where did you hear this?"

"From a member of Caesar's household, so it must be true."

"What do you think this means for us?"

"It's too early to say, but certainly it means an end to all of Domitianus's paranoid decrees and tribunals." He added, "Tell Prisca she's safe, at least for now!"

Slamming the door in his delight, Achilles ran through the house looking for Prisca, and found her with Julia in the *tablinum*. "Domina, Domina—great news! Domitianus is gone—killed! There will be no tribunal!"

---

[1] Domitian was assassinated on September 18, AD 96.

Prisca and Julia looked at each other in shock. Achilles was a formal man, but his delight overrode his sense of decorum, so all three spontaneously hugged and kissed each other, bouncing around the room in their delight and relief. None could really believe it to be true.

Finally Prisca stepped back and laughed gustily. "Well! Julia, I will remember to ask you to pray from now on when we have a crisis. The Lord clearly heard your supplication."

Julia laughed and clapped her hands. "Let's plan a festive dinner tonight. This calls for a celebration! Achilles, can you see to the details? But first tell us what happened."

He told them the little he knew about Domitianus's assassination and then rushed to attend to the details of the feast.

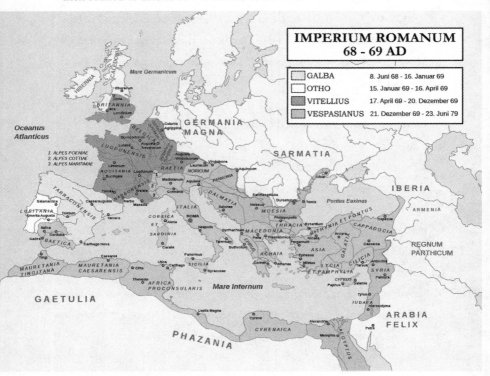

Figure 25.1. Map of the Roman Empire from AD 68-69.

After he left, Prisca paced the room a few more times before she finally settled into her chair. With a big sigh of relief she said, "Well, I thought our story would have to end there, but now I feel new vigor and hope that we can complete it."

Julia nodded, still ebullient in her excitement. She fairly ran to get her tablet, her smile still broad and joyful. When she returned, she asked with anticipation, "What do you want to tell next, now that we have all the time in the world?"

Prisca thought for a moment. "Where did we leave off?"

Julia looked down at her tablet. "You were going to tell us about Paulus's journeys to the East. I'm anxious to hear about that because I know nothing about it."

"Oh yes! Let's see." Prisca took a few breaths to calm down and switch her train of thought. She took a drink of wine to clear her throat and to force herself to relax. "Paulus received a distress letter from Timothy in Ephesus, and another from Titus in Crete. Poor Timothy. Paulus was his mentor, but he was not Paulus—he was timid, and the many strong personalities in Ephesus were difficult for him to deal with."

"Did Titus have the same problem?"

"No, Titus's problems had to do with starting assemblies in various places. But in both cases, Paulus helped them with the structure of their congregations, Prisca answered."

"Why was that so important?"

"Neither of them would be permanent residents of where they were, since Paulus counted on them to itinerate. So, it was important that the groups were in stable hands once the apostolic coworkers left."

"What were those structures?"

"He instructed them about setting up men as elders and deacons."

"No women?" Julia asked, since she'd begun thinking about this more. "You told me Paulus approved of women in leadership."

"That's true, but Paulus's pastoral principle was 'start with them where they are, and then lead them where you want them to go.' He knew the places Timothy and Titus served were male-dominated, especially on Crete, but if you carefully read the first letter Paulus wrote to Timothy, he mentions female deacons. Those texts were never meant to exclude women from praying or prophesying or teaching or whatever they were gifted and called by God to do. Paulus's view was to change those in the body of Christus over time rather than change society at large."

Julia thought about this for a moment, which led her to another question. "You said Luke stayed in Roma, so who wrote these letters for Paulus?"

"After Luke finished his second chronicle, he joined Paulus in Spain and then they traveled back to Ephesus together, where he wrote to Titus. Then they moved on to Macedonia, which is where Paulus wrote his first letter to Timothy. So I'm sure Luke did the writing. These last letters reflect his diction, style, and vocabulary. I like to say 'the hands are the hands of Luke, but the voice is the voice of Paulus.'[2] His eyesight by this point was about gone, especially due to the many times he had been stoned and beaten."

"So how did Paulus get back to Roma?"

"Someone in Macedonia, I think it was in Philippi, tipped off the authorities that Paulus was at the Lydian's house, and he was taken prisoner there and brought back to Roma. Faithful Luke traveled with him."

Prisca looked sad and reflective. "Paulus would write his last letter to Timothy from Roma, and this time the Roman judicial process would show no mercy. No one came to see Paulus because actually none of us knew where he was. The trial itself was a sham, a foregone conclusion."

"Did Peter ever meet Paulus in Roma?"

"Not to my knowledge. Paulus was in the Mamertine[3] as soon as he got back to Roma, and Peter was the first to go to be with the Lord. We should turn to that story now."

---

[2] An allusion to the story of Jacob and Esau.
[3] The prison was located on the northeastern slope of the Capitoline Hill.

Julia shuddered. "It's hard to talk about these things when you feel like you've narrowly escaped a similar fate."

Prisca nodded. "I know. I don't understand why some of us are spared and some are not."

Both women sat in respectful silence, pondering how each of them had providentially missed death. Finally, Julia broke the silence and asked, "Is it all right for me to rejoice in your freedom when others go to their demise?"

Prisca spoke up definitively. "Certainly! I've learned that each life spared is worth celebrating." She was quiet for a moment and added, "Especially if it's mine!"

At that both women laughed gently, breaking the tension enough to go on.

"Okay, on to Peter."

Prisca gave one firm nod and grew somber again. "Indeed. Peter was taken prisoner one morning in the catacombs. On that occasion, the authorities weren't interested in the rest of us. It was only three months after the fire in

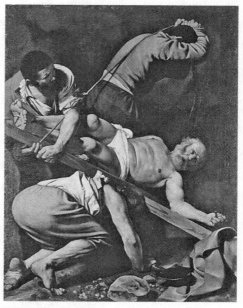

Figure 25.2. Michelangelo Caravaggio's famous portrait of the crucifixion of St. Peter.

Roma, when Nero had begun seeking out scapegoats from among the *Christianoi*. He was especially keen to make an example of the leaders, assuming the movement would suffer a deathblow. He could not have been more wrong. Martyrdom only strengthened the movement, as it was considered an honor to die in Jesus' name and in a manner like Jesus."[4] Prisca's voice grew softer. "Peter died that way, but inverted, on a cross."[5]

"Didn't Jesus warn Peter that he would come to an untimely end?[6] Julia asked, remembering an account she'd heard.

It took Prisca a moment to steady her voice. "He did indeed. He told him he'd be bound and led where he did not choose to go."

"Was it awful after that for believers?"

Prisca thought before answering. "It did frighten us. However, although the community of believers in Roma benefited from Peter's brief ministry, it wasn't founded by him nor did it founder when he was martyred. It carried on without strong leadership for a while. Considerably later, Clement became a great leader among us and still is today."

Prisca was quiet for a few moments until Julia asked, "What about Paulus?"

Prisca shook her head as if to clear her thoughts. "It didn't go well for him from the outset of the trial. As he says in his second letter to Timothy, 'At my first defense, no one came to my support, but everyone deserted me. May it not be held against them. But the Lord stood at my side and gave me strength, so that through me the message might be fully proclaimed and all the Gentiles might hear it. And I was delivered from the lion's mouth.'[7] I remember those words because they haunt me."

"Why did no one come?"

Prisca sighed. "The community didn't *know* the trial had begun. Those who knew deserted Paulus, except of course for Luke, and Luke had no time to seek us out. He was busy taking down what amounted to Paulus's

---

[4]Tertullian was later to say in about AD 197: "*Plures efficimur, quoties metimur a vobis; semen est sanguis christianorum.*" "We multiply whenever we are mown down by you; the blood of Christians is seed." *Apologeticus*, 50, s. 13.

[5]This is recorded in the later apocryphal work from the second century, the *Acts of Peter*. Perhaps a better source of information is Tertullian, who at the end of the second century AD, in his *Prescription Against Heretics*, notes that Peter endured a passion like his Lord's.

[6]John 21:18-19.

[7]2 Timothy 4:16-17.

last will and testimony, the second letter to Timothy, and tending to Paulus physically."

"So was Paulus eventually thrown to the lions?"

"I take his words as a reference to Nero himself. Paulus was surely beheaded, as befits a Roman citizen. And so ended the lives of our greatest apostles. Paulus contributed more to our community in Roma than Peter, but Peter was there at the crucial juncture to lead us into the catacombs, and to encourage us right after the fire. It was left to all of us to carry on, and the next person to do so in a crucial way was Mark, the sometime companion of both Paulus and Peter. We'll turn to his tale in the morning."

As they stood up and stretched, Prisca said, "Julia, I read very early this day in the Psalms that the mercies of the Lord are new every morning. I certainly feel his mercy today."

"Amen to that! Let's get ready for a festive meal."

However, after their happy meal, as Julia said her evening prayers, she thought of Domitianus. She prayed silently, *Master, you said we should love our enemies, and pray for those who persecute us, not rejoice in their murder. But, Lord, I can only feel elation right now. I hope that's all right.*

26

JOHN MARK AND THE ABOMINATION THAT MAKES DESOLATE

Julia was continually amazed at Prisca's ability to put hardship behind her and move ahead. Julia was still reeling from her emotions of the days before, but Prisca seemed to function as if she narrowly escaped death daily. She never mentioned anything about the day before but dived right into her account of when Jerusalem fell.

"Just when we thought things couldn't get much worse, we learned of the wars in the Promised Land. Now, with the benefit of hindsight, and having read Josephus's recently composed account *The Jewish War*, I realize the Jews had no chance against the might of Roma. But those tenacious zealots prolonged the inevitable many years. It took two Flavian Emperors, Vespasian and his son Titus, to finish the job."

Julia shook her head. "Yes, I always feel sad when I see the arch Titus built near the Colosseum. I can't help but mourn its depiction of the Roman triumphal procession bringing in spoils from the temple."

Prisca sighed, remembering her own life-changing visit to Jerusalem. "Yes, the Jewish people suffered much." She reflected for a moment before going

Figure 26.1. The burning of the temple in Jerusalem.

on. "This war and its outcome significantly changed Judaism. Formerly, it focused on Torah, temple, and territory. Now Judaism is a more Torah-centric religion. Gone are the Sadducees, Levites, and family of the high priests. Any hopes of independence are now mostly vain hopes. The religious landscape has changed dramatically."[1]

Prisca's thoughts flowed steadily. Since the trauma of having to testify had passed, she was better able to focus on the task at hand. The feast the previous night had been joyful and went on so long that no one in the household arose before midmorning. Even young Achilles slept late. So, Prisca hadn't started her story until the midday meal had been served. She was reclining on the couch, relaxed and sipping a little wine.

Julia hated to interrupt her, as she looked so content, but the younger woman had to ask about something she'd been wondering for some time. "How did we come to have this house?"

---

[1]Prisca was not quite right in some of this assessment. There was yet to be the Bar Kokhba revolt in the second century, and it would not be until AD 135 when the revolt was put down, and then Jerusalem was turned into a pagan city, *Aelia Capitolina*, and that plausible hope of having and running one's own country was snuffed out.

Figure 26.2. The Titus Arch.

Figure 26.3. A relief of the Titus Arch.

Prisca set her wine down and explored the past, trying to remember details. "It was the end of Nero's rule, and whether he killed himself or was killed, in any case he was gone. And one of the things frugal Vespasian did, after returning from Judaea and the war there, was to put several of Nero's properties up for sale.[2] This modest villa was available at that auction. Dear Aquila had left me a good amount of gold *aureii*, and I still had my dowry.

"The auction transpired in winter, a year and a half after Nero's death, and it was so cold that day many of the wealthy didn't show up or even send one of their agents. As providence would have it, those who did come wanted a much larger property than this villa."

Figure 26.4. The gold aureus, the most valuable of the Roman coins.

Prisca paused and looked over at Julia. "By then you were about nine, so I guess you remember moving here. Yes?"

"Oh yes. The day I had my own room, I could hardly contain my excitement. My friends at the tutor envied me."

Prisca couldn't help but smile at the thought of youthful Julia. "Thankfully, though Nero owned this property, he never lived here, so his *genius,* or spirit, has never haunted this place.[3] In fact, it had belonged to a well-off follower of Christus, from whom Nero had confiscated it."

"Thanks for telling me this story, Domina. I know it was an interruption, but I've always been curious. I should let you get back to the story. You mentioned Mark earlier. Can you tell me more?"

---

[2]Vespasian was very frugal. J. P. Morel, "The Craftsman," in *The Romans,* A. Giardina, ed. (University of Chicago Press, 1993), 228, tells the story of how an inventor presented Vespasian with a machine to hoist giant columns up to the Captoline at little cost to build—yet another monument with his name on it. Vespasian refused, saying "You must let me feed the common people (*plebiculam*)." Vespasian cut quite a different figure than, say, Nero, with his lavish spending and building aspirations.

[3]The word *genius,* from which we get *genie,* refers to the spirit of the ancestor—in this case, the master of the house.

Prisca nodded with a grin. "It's good for you to keep me on track." She thought a moment to pick up the chronicle at just the right place. "Peter was buried here in Roma in the cemetery on Vatican hill. Roman law forbad burying people within the city walls, but that hill was outside them. To this day, some followers of Christus go there and leave flowers remembering the man who has begun to be called Saint Peter.

"Anyway, Peter had given John Mark his notes on Jesus' story, as well as his sermons. At that time there was no written biography of Jesus. Mark was not highly trained in rhetoric, and his Greek was just simple and functional, sometimes reflecting the fact that he was thinking in Aramaic but writing in Greek. But Mark had enough elementary Greek education that he was able to form the stories about Jesus into *chreiae*.[4] There are a variety of these in Mark's account, which presents the story so that it builds up to, for example, Peter's recognition of Jesus as the Messiah, the Christus.[5] I take it that Mark's point is that until you know who Jesus is, you can't understand why he had to die on the cross.

"Toward the end of his narrative, Mark tells us that no one knows the timing of Christus's return—even Jesus didn't know while he walked this earth. However, in the third year of Pilate's reign, Jesus predicted the demise of the temple in Jerusalem within a generation. A Biblical generation is forty years, and so it's no accident the temple fell in AD 70.

"One of the more interesting features of that prophecy about the end of the temple, which is said to be part of the birth pangs of the beginning of the messianic age, not a harbinger of when Christus would return, is that Mark speaks of the 'abomination that causes desolation.'"[6]

"Yes. What is that referring to?"

---

[4]Forming *chreiae* was one of the regular exercises in elementary Greek education. They are brief reminiscences about an historical person, which usually end with a pithy saying, like "man is not made for the Sabbath but rather the Sabbath for man."
[5]Mark 8.
[6]Mark 13:14.

"Mark was alluding to the desecration of the temple by Antiochus Epiphanes, a desecration that sparked the Maccabean war.[7] Jewish followers of Jesus instantly recognized what he was speaking of. Jesus then suggested a similar desecration by a pagan was coming, and he was right."

"Did Mark write his account during the Jewish war?"

"Very perceptive of you, Julia! He did indeed. The Jewish war was raging, and the temple in Jerusalem would soon fall. Mark wanted the Roman audience to understand the significance of what was happening in Judaea, for the reports from there were intermittent, and with the demise of Nero that year, we had our own problems here in Roma."

"Domina, I've heard Mark's account described as stark and dark and even ominous at times."

"Yes, I've heard that too, but Mark does a good job making clear that the meaning of Christus and his work can only come when one accepts God's revelation about him. No one could arrive at those results by mere philosophy or logic because people weren't looking for a crucified and risen savior."

"You are right about that. Even Peter objected a moment after his great confession at Caesarea Philippi to Jesus' prediction of his own demise at the hands of the authorities."

"Good memory, Julia! Indeed, no one understood the meaning of it all until Jesus began to appear to various disciples. No one. Hindsight is a wonderful thing, but at least Jesus in his prophecies gave us some forewarning of what the future would look like, and of course he was right about Christus followers being dragged before officials and having to risk their lives to be faithful to Him."

Prisca sighed. "It's time to move beyond that tumultuous decade. And good riddance! Thankfully, things quieted for a *little* while after the fall of the temple in Jerusalem, but just when all seemed quiet on the western front of the empire, something totally unexpected erupted."

---

[7]Gentiles who had read the LXX of Daniel would recognize it as well.

27

TITUS RULES, AND THE VOLCANO ERUPTS

Ashes were already falling, not as yet very thickly. I looked round: a dense black cloud was coming up behind us, spreading over the earth like a flood. "Let us leave the road while we can still see," I said, "or we shall be knocked down and trampled underfoot in the dark by the crowd behind." We had scarcely sat down to rest when darkness fell, not the dark of a moonless or cloudy night, but as if the lamp had been put out in a closed room.

You could hear the shrieks of women, the wailing of infants, and the shouting of men; some were calling their parents, others their children or their wives, trying to recognize them by their voices. People bewailed their own fate or that of their relatives, and there were some who prayed for death in their terror of dying. Many besought the aid of the gods, but still more imagined there were no gods left, and that the universe was plunged into eternal darkness for evermore.

There were people, too, who added to the real perils by inventing fictitious dangers: some reported that part of Misenum had collapsed

or another part was on fire, and though their tales were false they
found others to believe them. A gleam of light returned, but we took
this to be a warning of the approaching flames rather than daylight.
However, the flames remained some distance off; then darkness came
on once more and ashes began to fall again, this time in heavy showers.
We rose from time to time and shook them off, otherwise we should
have been buried and crushed beneath their weight. I could boast
that not a groan or cry of fear escaped me in these perils, but I admit
that I derived some poor consolation in my mortal lot from the belief
that the whole world was dying with me and I with it.

PLINY THE YOUNGER'S
SECOND LETTER TO TACITUS, *EPISTLE* 6.20

JULIA CONTINUED TO WRITE AS PRISCA RESUMED: "Now that
we've talked about Mark, I would like to return to Luke. Luke spent much
of the next decade collecting his notes and revising his two volumes for
Theophilus. Though he had finished the first draft before going to Spain with
Paulus, when he came back he did more polishing—especially of the first
volume, which truly reflects his rhetorical skill."

"Who was Theophilus, Domina?"

"He was Luke's patron, and a new follower of Christus. Luke had many
concerns in writing his narrative, not the least of which was to make clear
that the movement had no desire to subvert the empire. This was no small
issue after the fire and the persecutions. In fact, Luke wrote the draft of his
second volume first, because Mark had already written his narrative of Jesus'
life, and Luke felt more need to tell the rest of the story. Then, using Mark
and several other sources, including a collection of Jesus' famous sayings, he
composed his own narrative of the good news."

"Is there a big difference between these two narratives of Jesus' life?"

"Interesting question . . ." Prisca answered, thinking as she spoke. "Mark wrote a biography of Jesus . . . but Luke wrote a Greek-styled historical work focusing on 'the things that have been fulfilled among us'[1] rather than focusing mainly on the character and characterization of Jesus, as Mark does."

Julia wrote furiously but still managed to ask another question. "What about the other documents about Jesus?"

"Let's see . . . in the eastern end of the empire, Matthew provided a good deal of material for the account attached to his name. He relied heavily on Mark's tale and presented a more Jewish portrait of Jesus than Luke did. That account was written for Jewish followers of Jesus in Galilee and perhaps Damascus and Antioch. I've not seen this work, but I understand it's full of teaching material to train disciples."

Julia wished she could read it. She had read the accounts they had so many times, she had great swaths of it memorized. "I wish we had that account, but I'm grateful you decided to fund the compiling of Paulus's letters into codex form all in one document. It will be so much easier to read that way."

"Yes. We realized after the persecutions that the apostles were disappearing, and we needed to be intent on collecting and copying the earliest documents from our movement so future *Christianoi* will have a good sense of what happened at the beginning."

"So, what happened to the Christus followers at this point?"

"Slowly, we began to grow again after the defections and deaths. Roma had other issues to deal with than us, thank goodness. The movement had spread to various towns in Italia, including Pompeii and Herculaneum. By the way, the followers of Jesus there had developed signals of where to meet. In Pompeii they used little reflective crosses to mark where their meetings were held, in the house of a baker, for instance.[2] In Herculaneum they used the *ichthus* symbol."

---

[1] Luke 1:1.

[2] On this, see Bruce W. Longenecker, *The Crosses of Pompeii* (Minneapolis, MN: Fortress Press, 2016).

"What's that?"

"Jesus talked about his followers being fishers of human beings, and the earliest ones were fishermen by trade. *Ichthus* is the Greek word for fish. But the ichthus symbol was in fact an abbreviated way of referring to *Iēsous christos theos uios sōtēr,* or 'Jesus Christus son of God savior.' This symbol seems to be popping up in various cities in the empire where there are *Christianoi;* for example, it can be seen scrawled on the wall in the market next to the harbor in Smyrna, with an arrow pointing the direction where you could find those who identified with this symbol."[3]

"How do you know about all these things?" Julia asked with wonder.

Prisca laughed. "I've been around a long time, and many believers have stayed in our home through the years as they traveled from these places. You've heard some of these stories too, but you were probably too young to remember them."

Julia gave a quick nod. "All the more reason to record them now!"

"Indeed. Now where was I? Oh yes. Toward the end of the decade, a gigantic, volcanic eruption in Pompeii buried Herculaneum with lava and Pompeii with soot and ash, killing hundreds of people. Pliny the Younger wrote an eyewitness account of this disaster.[4]

"It's hard to make clear what an incredible effect this event had on Roma in general, especially on the more superstitious. Was this some kind of punishment on Roma for something it did wrong, a punishment by an angry deity? Some of our fellow Christus followers thought God judged Roma for its treatment of us. The cities destroyed were wealthy and immoral, for they were where Romans went to play and to sun themselves in the nude and the like. Some likened this judgment to the story of Sodom and Gomorrah in the Scriptures."

---

[3] I have myself seen this at the archaeological dig in Izmir.

[4] This is an actual account of the event. Pliny *Epistulae* VI.16. I have quoted VI.20, a second letter, at the beginning of this chapter. The original is in Latin, but there are many translations available on the internet that are in the public domain. For an excellent historical novel about all that see Robert Harris, *Pompeii* (New York: Random House, 2005).

"What do you think?"

"I must confess, Julia, I have an issue with this suggestion. In the first place, many Christus followers died in this event. Furthermore, remember that Elijah is told that God is not in the wind, not in the earthquake, nor in the fire. One can only discern his will by listening to his still, small voice—his Word. So, I am skeptical of such interpretations. Was the fire in Roma a judgment of God on the poor in the *subura?* No, it was the result of intentional human wickedness."

"Thank you, Domina, for that explanation. I've puzzled over that for a long time and wondered what a Christus follower should think about the matter. How does God act in the world? Are all things fated or preordained? Does God work in the world by love and persuasion? What is it that Paulus used to say? 'In all things God works for the good of those who

Figure 27.1. Mount Vesuvius erupts.

love him.'[5] This doesn't mean everything that happens is good or from the hand of God. Isn't that right?"[6]

Prisca gave a definitive nod. "I agree. The living God is not like the pagan gods who are selfish, self-centered, all about their own needs and desires, and often irrational and immoral in their behavior, according to the Greek and Roman myths. This is nothing like the real God that we know in Christus, who loves us and gave himself up for us, even dying on a cross to cure us of our sin sickness."

Both women fell quiet as they pondered these great and weighty truths. Finally, Julia broke the silence. "How was the movement growing, and what were the difficulties?"

"Excellent question! But that needs to wait yet another day. We will talk about that in the morning. I'm suddenly feeling exhausted."

Hearing that, Julia stood and offered her mother her hand, which Prisca readily accepted. Julia was comforted that Prisca leaned her weight against her as they walked, Prisca now able to trust herself fully to her daughter's care.

---

[5]Romans 8:28.

[6]Some today have wondered if John of Patmos was reflecting a knowledge of this event in Revelation 16:17-21: "The seventh angel poured out his bowl into the air, and out of the temple came a loud voice from the throne, saying, 'It is done!' Then there came flashes of lightning, rumblings, peals of thunder and a severe earthquake. No earthquake like it has ever occurred since mankind has been on earth, so tremendous was the quake. The great city split into three parts, and the cities of the nations collapsed. God remembered Babylon the Great and gave her the cup filled with the wine of the fury of his wrath. Every island fled away and the mountains could not be found. From the sky huge hailstones, each weighing about a hundred pounds, fell on people. And they cursed God on account of the plague of hail, because the plague was so terrible." I would say probably Pompeii is not alluded to here because he is talking about things falling from the sky, not a mountain erupting.

28

"YOU MUST INCREASE, WHILE WE DECREASE"

Learn what are the merits of a concise book. This first—less of my paper is wasted, and then second my copiest gets through it in a single hour, and he will not be very busied with my trifles, the third thing then is this, that if you are read to anyone, bad as you may be all through, you will not bore. The guest will read you after his five measures [of wine] have been mixed and before the cup he puts aside begins to become cool. Do you think yourself protected by such brevity? Alas, to how many will you still seem long!

MARTIAL, *EPIGRAMS* 2.1

PRISCA STOOD IN THE GARDEN and inspected her spring flowers. She wanted to finish her chronicle, but this long story had taken a toll on her, and she was weary. In a sense, Prisca had always stood between two worlds, the Greco-Roman world and the world of early Judaism. Now in her eightieth year, she tried to understand what was happening to Jewish followers of Jesus. She felt great sorrow that they were diminishing.

To ponder this, she reread bits of Paulus's letter to the Romans, to help her understand why only a small minority of Jews followed Jesus. Even within the Jesus movement, the number of Jewish *Christianoi* became a smaller and smaller minority of the whole body of those who believed.

She had reached the point in Paulus's letters where he says,

> Brothers and sisters, my heart's desire and prayer to God for the Israelites is that they may be saved. For I can testify about them that they are zealous for God, but their zeal is not based on knowledge. Since they did not know the righteousness of God and sought to establish their own, they did not submit to God's righteousness. Christus is the end of the Mosaic law so that there may be righteousness for everyone who believes.[1]

And then a bit later in the discourse, he added:

> Again I ask: Did they stumble so as to fall beyond recovery? Not at all! Rather, because of their transgression, salvation has come to the Gentiles to make Israel envious. But if their transgression means riches for the world, and their loss means riches for the Gentiles, how much greater riches will their full inclusion bring! . . . If some of the branches have been broken off, and you, though a wild olive shoot, have been grafted in among the others and now share in the nourishing sap from the olive root, do not consider yourself to be superior to those other branches. If you do, consider this: You do not support the root, but the root supports you. You will say then, "Branches were broken off so that I could be grafted in." Granted. But they were broken off because of unbelief, and you stand by faith. Do not be arrogant, but tremble. For if God did not spare the natural branches, he will not spare you either. . . . I do not want you to be ignorant of this mystery, brothers and sisters, so that you may not be conceited: Israel has experienced a

---

[1]Romans 10:1-4.

hardening in part until the full number of the Gentiles has come in, and in this same way all Israel will be saved. As it is written:

"The deliverer will come from Zion;
> he will turn godlessness away from Jacob.
And this is my covenant with them
> when I take away their sins."[2]

Julia came upon Prisca as she read, so Prisca handed her the scroll. "Now if I am reading this right, we are now in the time of the Gentiles, and like the relationship between John the Baptizer and his cousin Jesus, *now* the Jews must decrease and the Gentiles increase according to the mysterious plan of God. *However*, and it is a big however, once the full number of Gentiles has been saved, then Christus will return, resurrect the dead, and then many Israelites will be saved. The phrase 'all Israel' in the Torah never means every Jew, but it does signal a large number. In other words, it will take nothing less than the return of the Jewish messiah for a large number of Jews to overcome their lack of faith in Him. It's clear that in this passage *Israel* refers to non-Christus following Jews. Is this how you would understand this passage?"

"Yes, Domina, I think that's right." Julia hesitated, still trying to grow in confidence as she had always deferred to her wiser elder. "But Jewish followers of Christus should not expect a large response to the good news from their kinsmen and kinswomen before Jesus himself calls Jews to repentance at the end of days."

Prisca visibly wilted. "I suppose it's easy to get caught up in visions of success."

Julia hated to see this strong woman lose hope. "In any case, we must do our best to witness and leave the results in God's hands."

"Excellent. You are so right. And we must be patient." Prisca's sharp mind kept spinning. "You will notice, however, two other things: Paulus says that

---

[2]Romans 11:11-12, 17-21, 25-27.

even pious Jews who are not Christus followers *need* to be saved, especially if they have heard and rejected the good news. Also, Christus fulfilled and brought to an end the Mosaic law and covenant, inaugurating a new covenant."

"So the Mosaic covenant is obsolete?"

"Yes. This is something many Jewish followers of Jesus have *not* understood, and it's one of the reasons some of them have vehemently opposed Paulus's message and teaching on this subject. On one hand, God is not finished with Israel, but on the other hand, the Mosaic covenant is now obsolete. It's an already and not yet situation. The Judaizers who so plagued Paulus many years ago saw the Jesus movement as simply the messianic form of Judaism and its Mosaic covenantal practices. Paulus hoped Jew and Gentile would unite in Christus by grace through faith in Jesus."

Julia puzzled. "Paulus's letters are complex."

Prisca chuckled. "They certainly are! That's one reason I love to keep reading them over. They challenge me."

"Have we left any letters out of our account?"

"Yes. Jacob, Jesus' brother, wrote a beautiful sermon to the Jewish followers of Jesus in the Diaspora. He alludes to many of the core wisdom sayings of Jesus, trying to get Jewish believers in Jesus to behave like Jesus said we should—taming our tongues, overcoming temptation, doing good works of many sorts, including caring for the poor, confessing our sins to each other, and more. But even Jacob doesn't really delineate what our praxis should be when it comes to many issues—but then he hardly needs to rehearse the Torah since he wrote to Jews."

"You still look weary, Domina." Julia took the scroll Prisca had handed her and pointed to the flowers of Prisca's garden. "Let's call it a day and simply rest, and enjoy the beauties of this creation God has given us. Together."

"My, my, daughter," Prisca said, with a wink. "You are becoming rather wise in your old age."

29

UNNERVED NERVA AND THE END OF DAYS

Agricola was spared those later years during which Domitianus,
leaving now no interval or breathing space of time, but, as it were, with
one continuous blow, drained the life-blood of the Commonwealth.
. . . It was not long before our hands dragged Helvidius to prison,
before we gazed on the dying looks of Manricus and Rusticus, before
we were steeped in Senico's innocent blood. Even Nero turned his eyes
away, and did not gaze upon the atrocities which he ordered; with
Domitianus it was the chief part of our miseries to see and to be seen,
to know that our sighs were being recorded.

TACITUS, *AGRICOLA* 44-45

JULIA FELT DEEP CONTENTMENT and satisfaction. Today, they would wrap up Prisca's story. They rose early in anticipation, and her mother wasted no time getting into her narrative.

"I've been giving much thought to Domitianus since his demise. There is no doubt he was a tyrant, and a rather paranoid one as well. But there was a sort of ruthless efficiency to his autocratic rule. What he couldn't tolerate was dissent—in particular, dissent from the imperial cult. He demanded to be worshiped as *Deus et dominus noster*—'God and our Lord,' which followers of Christus could not in good conscience do. Many actually came to see Domitianus as a second or third Nero, back from the dead,[1] which is part of the reason I was summoned to his tribunal."

"How did you stay so calm during all that uncertainty, Domina?"

Prisca didn't answer for a while. She seemed to be pulling all her years of wisdom together into her reply. "I've learned the meaning of Paulus's words when he said that God works all things together for good for those who love him. How can I not marvel that on the very day I was called to testify at the tribunal, the tyrant was assassinated, killed by his own entourage of court officials, some of the household of Caesar."

"Domina, I've been worrying about that. Were any of the Christus followers a part of that assassination?"

Prisca shook her head resolutely. "None! And I do mean none. Christus followers disliked Domitianus, but they would never participate in the plot to do away with the emperor. They followed our master's teaching to do no harm, and even to love our enemies and pray for them."

Julia nodded, feeling herself relax as that worry dissipated. "Didn't John of Patmos allude to Domitianus as Nero back from the dead in his apocalyptic prophecies written for the Asian assemblies?"[2]

"I've heard of such. The senate despised Domitianus almost as much as did John of Patmos, declaring *Damnatio memoriae*.[3] This included the senate ordering the immediate melting down of all coins with that emperor's face on it, and the destruction of his statues in Roma, though I'm not sure this order will be carried out."

---

[1] On this, see the excellent novel by Lindsey Davis, *The Third Nero* (New York: Minotaur Books, 2017).
[2] Revelation 13:5-18.
[3] Which means that his memory was assigned to oblivion, forever.

"What do you make of Nerva, who has succeeded Domitianus?"

"It's too soon to tell. This certainly ends the Flavian dynasty. Nerva is an old man and hardly up to the task of being emperor. He's old, childless, and has spent his life out of the public's eye, rather like Claudius who was more of a scholar than a politician."

Julia nodded in agreement. "What a tumultuous century this has been!"

"It certainly has. Against many odds, the followers of Christus have increased dramatically since his death in Jerusalem. Here in Roma, the congregations of Christus followers existed before Paulus or Peter ever arrived in Roma; the assemblies survived the Neronian persecutions after the fire, survived the death of the two famous apostles, survived further trials and tribulations including the obliteration of numerous Christus followers due to Vesuvius's eruption, and now we have also survived Domitianus—including me, who escaped at the last minute."

Julia looked down at the many words she'd written. In a soft voice, she asked what she'd been wondering since they began their task. "What will happen to our document, Domina?"

"Here in Roma, Clement has been collecting various early documents from our movement, and perhaps this chronicle will be added. But, quite honestly, I don't care what becomes of it. I somehow feel relieved that the story has left me and that you got to hear all of it. That may be enough.

"Telling this story has reminded me of what Jesus himself said—that the gates of Hades, and so of death, will not prevail against Christus's body. It will go on until the thief in the night returns to claim this world, and the kingdoms of this world become the kingdoms of our God and of his Christus. Oh, Julia, how I long for that day!"

"Amen and amen," Julia said as she put her stylus down, adding with a smile, "We have fought the good fight, run the good race, and we have finished with a chronicle in our hands."

Prisca grinned, proud of her protégé. "Yes, my Julia. This story began with fire from heaven in Jerusalem, continued with fire in Roma and in southern Italia, and Roma is still burning today, but now with the fire of Spirit, not with the earthly fires of emperors. And no one shall ever put out this flame. No one. Even the eternal flame in the Temple of the Vestal Virgins has gone out occasionally, but not this flame of the Spirit."

Julia took a deep breath and said, "Time to go buy extra bottles of ink, more papyri, and to sharpen my stylus. I have many days of writing to make a fair hand copy of this chronicle. But . . . it will be worth it."

And with that, Julia and Prisca embraced and held one another, as they watched the sun set over the Esquiline Hill, heading west, as would the movement itself.[4]

---

[4]It is also true that the church was growing in the east as well, but Prisca's sources on that fact were few after the destruction of the temple in AD 70.

IMAGE CREDITS

Figure 1.1. Map by Jeanna Wiggins, © InterVarsity Press

Figure 1.2. Greg Willis / Wikimedia Commons

Figure 2.1. RonGafni / Wikimedia Commons

Figure 2.2. Carole Raddato / Wikimedia Commons

Figure 2.3. Peter van der Sluijs / Wikimedia Commons

Figure 2.4. Naples National Archaeological Museum, Carole Raddato / Wikimedia Commons

Figure 2.5. Sodabottle / Wikimedia Commons

Figure 4.1. Archäologische Staatssammlung München, Mattes / Wikimedia Commons

Figure 5.1. GerardM / Wikimedia Commons

Figure 6.1. J. W. Mollett, *An Illustrated Dictionary of Words Used in Art and Archaeology* (London: Sampson Low, Marston, Searle, and Rivington, 1883) / Wikimedia Commons

Figure 6.2. Davide Mauro / Wikimedia Commons

Figure 6.3. Erik Drost / Wikimedia Commons

Figure 6.4. West Yorkshire Archaeology Advisory Service, Amy Downes / Wikimedia Commons

Figure 6.5. Photo by the author

Figure 7.1. Matthias Hollander / Wikimedia Commons

Figure 7.2. Naples National Archaeological Museum, Marie-Lan Nguyen / Wikimedia Commons

Figure 7.3. Altes Museum / Wikimedia Commons

Figure 8.1. Erik Cleves Kristensen / Wikimedia Commons

Figure 8.2. Photo by the author

Figure 8.3. Julian Fong / Wikimedia Commons

Figure 8.4. Nikater / Wikimedia Commons

Figure 11.1. Norman Herr / Wikimedia Commons

Figure 11.2. Public domain / Wikimedia Commons

Figure 14.1. Hanay / Wikimedia Commons

Figure 15.1. Sean Hayford O'Leary / Wikimedia Commons

Figure 15.2. Photo by the author

Figure 17.1. Sputnikcccp / Wikimedia Commons

Figure 17.2. Photo by the author

Figure. 17.3. Photo by the author

Figure 18.1. British Library, photo by the author

Figure 18.2. British Library, public domain / Getty Images

Figure 18.3. Römischer Schuh (RGM Köln), MrArifnajafov / Wikimedia Commons

Figure 18.4. Carole Raddato / Wikimedia Commons

Figure 21.1. *The Fire of Rome, 18 July 64 AD*, by Hubert Robert, Musee of Modern Art André Malraux / Wikimedia Commons

Figure 21.2. *Nero, and the Burning of Rome*, Quo Vadis, Altemus edition, 1897, illustration by M. de Lipman / Wikimedia Commons

Figure 22.1. Public domain / Wikimedia Commons

Figure 23.1. *The Christian Martyrs' Last Prayer* by Jean-Léon Gérôme (1863), Walters Art Museum / Wikimedia Commons

Figure 25.1. Andrei nacu / Wikimedia Commons

Figure 25.2. *Crucifixion of St. Peter* by Michelangelo Caravaggio (1600) / Wikimedia Commons

Figure 26.1. *The Siege and Destruction of Jerusalem* (1850) by David Roberts / Wikimedia Commons

Figure 26.2. Alexander Z / Wikimedia Commons

Figure 26.3. Gunnar Bach Pedersen / Wikimedia Commons

Figure 26.4. Gift of Joseph H. Durkee, 1899, Metropolitan Museum of Art / Wikimedia Commons

Figure 27.1. *An Eruption of Vesuvius Seen from Portici* by Joseph Wright of Derby, Huntington Library, Pasadena, CA / Wikimedia Commons

Also Available from IVP Academic

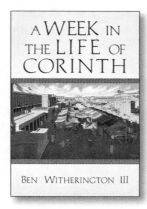

A WEEK IN THE LIFE OF CORINTH

BEN WITHERINGTON III

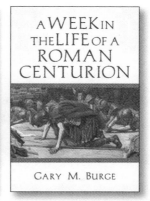

A WEEK IN THE LIFE OF A ROMAN CENTURION

GARY M. BURGE

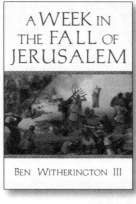

A WEEK IN THE FALL OF JERUSALEM

BEN WITHERINGTON III

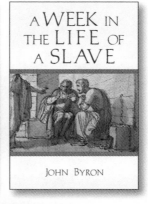

A WEEK IN THE LIFE OF A SLAVE

JOHN BYRON

PAULA GOODER

PHOEBE

A Story

Finding the Textbook You Need

The IVP Academic Textbook Selector
is an online tool for instantly finding the IVP books
suitable for over 250 courses across 24 disciplines.

ivpacademic.com